Roach - Text copyright © Emmy Ellis 2024
Cover Art by Emmy Ellis @ studioenp.com © 2024

All Rights Reserved

Roach is a work of fiction. All characters, places, and events are from the author's imagination. Any resemblance to persons, living or dead, events or places is purely coincidental.

The author respectfully recognises the use of any and all trademarks.

With the exception of quotes used in reviews, this book may not be reproduced or used in whole or in part by any means existing without written permission from the author.

Warning: The unauthorised reproduction or distribution of this copyrighted work is illegal. No part of this book may be scanned, uploaded, or distributed via the Internet or any other means, electronic or print, without the author's written permission

ROACH

Emmy Ellis

Chapter One

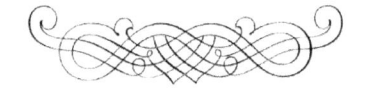

On a roasting July evening, Roach lounged at the kitchen table in the flat where he conducted the finer points of his business. He needed privacy for some things with the only two people he trusted. They knew exactly how far he was prepared to go. He lived two lives, never the twain shall meet if he could help it. He was used to that, being more than one person. He'd had to do it throughout his childhood.

A memory came, the one that always intruded whenever he thought about being a kid. There were many more, but that one… God, he'd need hypnotherapy to get rid of it. Or maybe it wasn't the memory itself that bothered him but the associated guilt he tried so hard to bury. How the fuck did it still get to him now, all these years later?

You should have been a better person. Should have gone to the police, even before it all happened. It would have stopped—

But would it? Nah, he doubted it. Things would have ended with the same result, just via a different route.

He flicked the memory away.

His second-in-command, Boycie, sat opposite, digging the point of a wooden toothpick between his molars. They'd known each other since primary school and were now out to make the best living they could, no matter who they hurt in the process. Boycie had become a brother—blood meant nothing, as Roach knew full well—and they shared the same outlook on life for the most part. Although Boycie had more of a conscience when it came to women.

They'd just eaten steak and chips, cooked by the tart who rented the place from Roach and was his main eyes and ears. Precious, a bit of a tasty bird, had legs for miles and long hair. Pretty thing. She'd taken the edge off since Roach's missus, Alice, had fucked off, running scared, all because he'd lumped her one when she hadn't behaved. She didn't know he knew where she was, but he was nothing if not resourceful, and he had the money to grease the palms of those who'd told him where she'd gone. Her mates. Seemed loyalty in friendship wasn't high on their priority list. They'd thrown Alice to the big bad wolf.

If Boycie and Precious ever did that to me, if they cross me, I'll kill them.

Intel had come in ages ago to confirm Alice was at a refuge, Dolly's Haven. Kayla Barnes had done a brilliant job of infiltrating the place, her boyfriend, Cooper, an invaluable asset, if a bit of a wannabe drug dealer. Kayla, pretending to be someone called Vicky, had gone to Haven and asked to be allowed in, running from her partner, 'Parker'. If The Brothers had done checks to see if a Vicky Hart actually existed, they'd have found a match—her details belonged to some woman from Essex. As Vicky, Kayla had spun the story she'd moved to London for her job with Parker, then things had gone tits up.

As payment for their time and effort, Roach had offered them one of his flats to rent for cheap in the same block as this one. Cooper had been stupid enough to run drugs from Kayla's rented house, and someone had grassed on them to the landlord. They'd been kicked out, sofa-surfing until Roach had gone up to them in the Horse and Hounds, asking them to help him out. Kayla had moved into Haven, and Cooper had stayed with a mate until the job was complete. Now they lived in the flat.

As Roach, a drug king who'd so far stayed beneath the twins' radar, he skated close to the wind. Risked getting caught. The Brothers couldn't be as savvy as the rumours said if they hadn't cottoned on to what he was up to. He paid no protection money—fuck that—and the thrill of his job was like no other. Boycie had said Roach's arrogance would get him killed one day, and maybe he was right. Roach would have a fucking good life in the meantime, though.

In his other life, he was Everett who owned a nice four-bed semi in a respectable street with respectable neighbours. A man so worried about his ex-wife going missing that the residents had taken to bringing meals round, like she was dead or something.

She would be soon.

Precious leaned her arse on the sink unit, her arms folded. "How much am I getting paid for my part in this again?"

"You know how much."

"Yeah, but I like hearing you say it."

Roach sighed. "A year's free rent."

"And how come?" She smiled.

He'd indulge her. "I suppose you like hearing about that, too, don't you. By paying you that way, a poke into my bank accounts by coppers means no lump sum withdrawal will point to me arranging this." He shook his head. "You're sick, keep wanting me to repeat this."

She laughed. "Tell me something I don't know…like where I'm meant to shoot her."

"It's got to be the forehead. Several shots."

Precious nodded. "I've had a walk round the outside of Haven, and there's a high brick wall surrounding the place. How, exactly, do you expect me to kill her if I can't get inside?"

"That's where my genius comes in, and I left this part of the plan out on purpose until we're ready to go. But I may as well tell you now." Roach straightened his tie. As far as his neighbours, Alice, and the twins were concerned, he was a high-flying businessman in the financial world. The suits, ties, fancy shoes, the house, and his expensive car helped create that illusion. When out as Roach, he preferred trackie bottoms and hoodies, his face hidden by a mask and sunglasses, his hair covered up. "Kayla's going to send a message, get Alice to meet her. Haven's monitored, there's cameras there, so she'll be seen going out, but whatever. All you need to do is shoot her at the meet location then make yourself scarce."

"Where's the location?"

"Curls and Tongs hair salon."

Precious raised her eyebrows. "That's where I go to get my barnet done. The Brothers are there a lot."

Roach pondered that. "Reckon they own it?"

"No, a woman called Stacey does—I asked, as you do. Maybe she borrowed money off them to afford the lease and that's why they keep turning up, to collect repayments."

"Maybe." Roach picked up his plate and held it out to her. "You'll do it on a motorbike. It'll be left round the back of this block by the communal wheelie bins along with a helmet. Boycie's going to nick some leathers off a mate."

Precious took his plate. "Right."

He'd known her since school, too, had a proper crush on her once upon a time, his teenage hormones running riot. He'd contemplated going steady with her, but she was too much of a live wire for him to have around permanently. He didn't like strong women, not as a partner. Alice had been the quiet and shy type, perfect, and he'd engineered it so she'd done whatever he'd said without realising he'd manipulated her. But the stupid cow had buddied up with those two friends of hers he'd paid off, and they'd convinced her to leave him.

Alice had gone into hiding for the first time. The letter asking for a divorce had angered him, but he'd granted it, willing to play the long game, to hold on to his revenge until the time was right. They might not have been man and wife any longer, but he'd found her in her little bolthole and turned up to give her a good wallop. He'd visited her a few nights, and the stupid cow had opened the door each time. He had no sympathy for anyone who invited a punch. Then she'd run to Haven.

And here we are.

He admired Precious' backside as she washed up his and Boycie's plates. Boycie did, too, and they shared a smile.

"Don't even think about it until I'm done," Roach warned him quietly.

"Yep, but when you are, it's fair game."

Roach nodded. Boycie was welcome to her after Roach had found another woman.

The other side of his business, a sex empire, was going from strength to strength. He didn't give two shits that he wasn't allowed to run such a business on Cardigan unless he had the twins' permission—or that he was in direct competition with Debbie at The Angel. He paid the rent on a house, ten bedrooms, and it was known by those who worked for him as the Orange Lantern on account of the coloured bulb in the light casing beside the front door. The nearest neighbours were about a quarter of a mile away.

"What are you two on about now?" Precious asked over her shoulder.

"Nothing," Boycie said. "Got any pudding?"

"Greedy bastard. I can make you an Eton mess."

Boycie laughed. "A growing man's got to eat." He cocked his head at Roach. "Now don't bite my head off, and I rarely butt in, but in all seriousness, is killing Alice necessary?"

Here we go. His conscience has kicked in.

Boycie had a soft spot for Alice. They'd got along well, her thinking he was Roach's right-hand man at his pretend, legal business. He'd come round for dinner sometimes while Roach and Alice had been married, and they'd talked bullshit about Roach's non-existent company to bolster the illusion. Alice had swallowed the lot, never asking questions. That had been novel; most women would have asked what he did at the dating stage, but her? Nah, she'd accepted the bare minimum he'd told her. That's when he'd known she was perfect for him.

He cleared his throat. "If I've said I want her shooting, then yeah, it's necessary. I don't say this crap for the fun of it."

"So even though the twins are at Haven a lot, as Kayla's told you, and they're on hand for all the women no matter what, you're willing to risk them finding out it's you who ordered the hit? At a hair salon they *also* visit a lot? I mean, have you got a death wish?"

Roach drummed his fingertips on the table. "I see where you're coming from, but she pissed me off and needs to pay for it. Death might be an over-the-top reaction in your eyes, but this bollocks didn't happen to you, did it, it happened to me. I've always meted out justice as I saw fit."

"But the only 'crime' she committed was leaving you because you hit her. It's her right not to get punched or slapped."

"We're never going to agree on some things, Boycie, and this is one of them, which is why I didn't ask *you* to shoot her, because I knew you wouldn't. You've got weird ideas about what women should and shouldn't put up with."

"I don't agree a man—or woman—has the right to beat their other half up just because they feel like it. I watched my dad do it to my mum for years until I grew up enough to give him a good hiding."

"So you've told me a million times. Some women deserve it, though—I can't be wrong, else there wouldn't be places like Haven, would there? Loads of people whack their partners on the daily."

"But Haven and the like shouldn't have to exist," Boycie said. "If people kept their slaps and fists to themselves, no one would need to run there. I can see it's not going in your head and I'm wasting my fucking breath."

"Thank fuck for that. Maybe you'll shut up now."

Precious poured the bubbly water out of the bowl and turned to lean on the sink unit. She dried a plate with a tea towel that had a hole in the corner. "Don't get me wrong, I'll do whatever for a year's free rent, but what did Alice actually *do* that warrants death? I think that's what Boycie can't get his head around."

Roach didn't expect them to understand how all the things Alice had done wormed inside his mind and created a hatred for her so deep that he couldn't stand the thought of her breathing for much longer. She'd disobeyed him. Run. Sent divorce papers. Run again. She hadn't stayed for the duration, she'd left him when it had got tough. Like Mum. Fuck, he wasn't going into that at the minute.

"She's done loads of stuff." He sniffed. "They all added up. I thought you were making Eton mess anyway?"

"Just about to." Precious took strawberries out of the fridge. "You'll have to wash the bowls out after because I need to get to the Lantern in a sec. That new tart's coming for her interview at seven."

Roach nodded. "Don't worry, then. We'll go down to that new shop, Pudding Place."

Boycie shot to his feet. "I've heard they do nice shit there. Biscoff this an' that."

Roach stood. "See you later, Precious."

She nodded.

They left, Roach's mind on fucking her later, Boycie's undoubtedly on Biscoff this an' that. Roach got in his 'other life' car, something he'd been bringing here since he'd found out he was likely being watched by the twins. He needed it seen outside the block of flats regularly so George and Greg thought he'd moved on from Alice by seeing Precious.

Like fuck have I.

Chapter Two

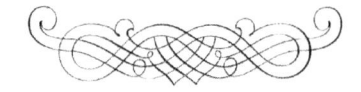

Another bloody hot day, Kayla's skin sticky from sweat, although she'd used liquid talc beneath her tits and between her legs. Maybe she ought to cover her whole body with the stuff. The weather had been so shite until recently, but the sun had finally decided to burn everyone with a vengeance this past week. Climate change really was a thing, then. Kayla was sick of hearing about it. Dad reckoned she ought to care, seeing as by the time she was his age, the floods and whatever would be much worse, but she lived in a flat so it wouldn't affect her. She'd tried to give a fuck about a lot of things, but it never worked. All she was bothered about was what she got out of life—and that was selfish, apparently, but she was who she was. No amount of pep talks from her parents throughout the years had changed her ways. She'd accepted she could be spiteful and was only out for herself, and the sooner others stopped trying to change her, the better things would be.

A message had come through on the WhatsApp group last night from Everett, that bugging woman, Edna, rushing to answer him straight away like a little creep. He'd said his girlfriend, Precious, the woman who lived in a flat along the balcony, was on board to kill Alice.

Kayla didn't give a shit about how she, herself, was integral to the murder going ahead, how it was wrong, blah, blah, blah. He'd instructed her to text Alice to arrange a meet—one o'clock was the time Alice had agreed to check the secret phone every day, the one Kayla had left behind so they could keep in contact.

Would Alice have the guts to leave Haven, though, even for an hour or two? Would the promise of a new hairdo be enough to lure her out? God knew the woman needed one. Loads of split ends, and her roots were hideous. The women were advised not to leave without an escort until their abusers had been spoken to or beaten up by the twins, but in Kayla's opinion, if they wanted to go out, it was their choice.

The twins looked into every abuser, had men watching them, and as far as Kayla knew, they still thought Everett was a businessman who had a woman on the side—Precious. Would they warn her about him? Say he was a fisty arsehole? If they did, at least Precious could tell Everett to be extra vigilant. He was already careful, what with Kayla telling him he was being observed. But how would he explain going to the Orange Lantern if they asked him? She supposed he could make out he was shagging one of the women, but then that might bring to light the fact it was a brothel. George and Greg would be livid if they knew a secret business was on the go.

Widow ran it, her name on the tenancy agreement, but Everett paid the rent and bills, so if the twins poked about there, Widow would get the blame for running a knocking shop. She risked getting a Cheshire for working on Cardigan without permission or paying protection money, all for the large wage she received each week. Kayla could see the draw. Cash was king. Maybe she could speak to Everett about running her own brothel so he could expand his empire.

She was chuffed that he'd confided in her about so many things. Maybe he saw potential in her. Or maybe he was testing her to see if she could keep her gob shut.

She glanced around the office. She hated being back at work. She'd taken a lot of time off to go and stay at Haven, making out to her doctor she was ill so she'd get a note then sick pay. She'd played the depression card and taken the monthly prescriptions for diazepam to the chemist. Those tablets were then sold to Everett who said he had a dealer mate he could pass them on to. She'd made a nice little profit. Bought herself a Radley handbag and a pair of Prada shoes and everything.

The tapping of nails on keyboards seemed louder today, more irritating. People here did her head in, all pious about certain things. Like drugs. And Cooper. None of her colleagues liked her boyfriend, they'd made that pretty clear, and to be fair, she could see why. He'd been an arrogant twat when he'd joined them for drinks after work last week. He sold drugs and was a bit of a dick, but he was nice to Kayla, and that was the most important thing, wasn't it? He didn't slap her around, he loved her evil streak, and she'd never be running scared like those stupid, gullible cows at Haven. Like Alice.

God, that woman was such a wet lettuce. She'd cried a lot, her story about Everett so pitiful that everyone else felt sorry for her. As Vicky, Kayla had pretended to care and, of course, she'd had her own story to tell about 'Parker'. They'd swallowed it, even The Brothers, which had surprised her. It had worried her that they'd recognise her, despite the red wig and glasses. All right, it was a bang-up disguise from Everett and she'd spoken with an Essex accent while at their precious refuge, but fucking hell, she'd had to be on constant alert in case she slipped up.

The encounter she'd had with them before going to Haven had unnerved her, something that didn't happen often. It had pissed her off that they'd had the ability to send her cold with fear.

The rumours were all true — the twins didn't fuck about, especially George, who'd threatened to slice her face if she lied about a man touching her up again. It had only been something to pass the time in the Noodle and Tiger, making out that bloke had pinched her bum. If only she hadn't mucked it up when speaking to George and Greg, saying he'd groped her tit, then she'd never have been scared out of her mind.

She'd admit that seeing them after that, the day she'd gone to Haven for 'help', she'd wished, if only for a smidgen of time, that she hadn't agreed to help Everett. That she was getting in way over her head. But she'd lost her home, and when he'd overheard that in the pub and said he could help them if they helped him... She'd have been a fool to turn that down, a flat with half-price rent for a year.

It wasn't until she'd gone to Haven that she'd found out Everett wasn't who she'd thought. You know, some rich bloke arsey with his ex-wife. Cooper had got a kid to follow Everett, and it turned out he was some fella people were proper wary of. The kid reckoned he was called Roach. That had always been just a name to Kayla before, one whispered on the Estate, so to know his actual identity was something Kayla and Cooper could use to their advantage later if they needed to. From what she'd heard, Roach was an absolute maniac.

On second thought, maybe she shouldn't cross him.

When she'd got the message from Cooper on her secret phone about the Roach/Everett thing, she'd wanted to run from Haven. To abandon the job. A rock and a hard place had sprung to mind. But she'd have been homeless if she hadn't gone through with it. Still, that was all in the past. The flat was lush, and Cooper had been busy building furniture, all IKEA. Mum and Dad hadn't been round yet, and she doubted they'd bother. Dad had had enough of Kayla's lies, and Mum was apparently worn out with all the 'drama'.

Fucking hell, parents were such nosy bastards, weren't they, thinking they had the right to butt in all the time. Kayla was an adult, and they needed to mind their own sodding business, especially since she'd moved out from under their roof.

They'd have egg on their faces soon enough. She'd prove she could stand on her own two feet, even though they'd shaken their heads at her about losing the rented house, something they'd predicted. All right, she had Cooper helping her this time, but she didn't have to rely on her parents anymore. And if they didn't like the devil spawn they'd created, that was their problem.

She checked the clock on the wall above her desk. Lunchtime, only two minutes away. She saved then closed the document she'd worked on all morning and set her computer to sleep. Got up at the same time as the woman next to her, one of those extra-virtuous types who thought her shit didn't stink. Kayla left the office, nipping across the street to the little shop. She bought a meal deal then walked down the road, turning into an alley that led to a park, a housing estate beyond. She sighed at the amount of people there. Didn't the lazy wankers have jobs?

The shriek of kids set her nerves on edge more than the clacking of the keyboards at work. Who the hell would want children? The snotty-nosed fuckers had never appealed. She'd be a crap mum anyway, too selfish, something Mum had reminded her of time and time again, but at least Kayla was big enough to acknowledge that. Cooper didn't want children either. Bonus.

She sat as far away from the brats as possible, beneath a tree, glad of the cooling shade. She had twenty-odd minutes to waste before Alice would check the phone, but she typed out a message now.

VICKY: GOT A NICE SURPRISE FOR YOU. CAN YOU GET OUT OF HAVEN FOR THE MORNING TOMORROW? I'LL WAIT OUT THE FRONT FOR YOU SO YOU DON'T HAVE TO WORRY ABOUT BEING ALONE. LET ME KNOW IF IT'S SAFE TO RING YOU WHEN YOU'VE READ THIS SO WE CAN DISCUSS THE DEETS.

She opened her sandwich and bottle of Coke. Stared at a boy who'd kicked his football towards her. He was about three, chubby-as-eff legs, and she wanted to slap his podgy cheek. The mother ran to collect him, giving Kayla an apologetic gesture, then picked the lad up, forgetting his ball. The boy wailed.

Shut the fuck up, you whinging little bastard.

She got up and walked to another tree, farther from the children, settling down to eat her egg and cress sarnie. Nosed around while she ate. Two men stood by the gates to her left, doing the drug handshake, and some scruffy pleb staggered past them, likely pissed as a fart. He lurched to a bench and flopped on it, facedown.

Parts of Cardigan really were bad. Kayla loved the Estate but at the same time wished for better things. Money, cars, clothes, and with Cooper, she was going to get it. He wasn't coining it in just yet, hence why they'd agreed to help Everett so they could get the flat, but he'd get there. They'd live the high life eventually. She planned to get Everett to employ them permanently. After all, they'd shown him they were people he could trust. She wanted more than her current wage from her shitty desk job.

Her message alert went off earlier than expected, and she checked her phone.

ALICE: CAN'T RING, TOO MANY PEOPLE AROUND. THE NEW COOK KEEPS LOOKING AT ME EVERY TIME I USE THIS PHONE. IT'S NOT LIKE WE'RE NOT ALLOWED THEM, IS IT. SHE'S NOTHING LIKE LUCIA. IT'S AS IF SHE DOESN'T WANT TO BE HERE.

Maybe she didn't. Roach could have twisted her arm, giving her no choice but to work there.

Kayla thought back to the old cook, Lucia, who'd overheard her conversation with Alice that time. Kayla had said she was going to kill Parker, and Lucia had given some unsolicited advice. The fact that Kayla *wasn't* going to kill Parker was by the by, it was a just a cover to ensure she fitted in at Haven, but still, the old goat butting in had naffed her off.

Vicky: Lucia was a well nosy cow. So, about the surprise. Are you up for it?

Alice: Depends what it is.

Vicky: It won't be a surprise if I tell you.

Alice: But you know how nervous I get about Everett seeing me. I swear he's watching me, or he's got someone else to do it.

Vicky: Okay, I'll tell you. It's just a visit to the hairdresser, all right? The Brothers are at the salon a lot, you know, Curls and Tongs? If you're that worried, ask them to be there. Your appointment is at ten. Come on, please say yes. New hair will make you feel better about yourself, maybe some acrylic nails, too.

Alice: But Stacey comes here to do hair. Why can't I wait until then?

Vicky: Because you need to get out of that place for a bit. It isn't healthy to be cooped up all the time.

Alice: Will we get a taxi?

Vicky: Yep. See you in the morning.

Alice: xxx

That sorted, Kayla ate her slice of chocolate brownie and spent the rest of her break sipping Coke and imagining ways to dispose of all those kids. She wasn't right in the head, she knew that well enough, but it was fun to entertain the intrusive thoughts that entered her mind a lot of the time. Dad had said she needed to see a psychiatrist, and the twins provided therapy sessions with some old bloke, which she'd had at Haven, but as she didn't feel her thoughts were a problem, why bother to continue seeing him?

The three-year-old headed towards her again, his mother too busy chatting to another woman to notice where he was going, laughing about something or other. Kayla could pick him up and walk off with him if she wanted to, her hand across his mouth to muffle his scream. Another gate was nearby. She could take him to the flat. Lock him in the smallest bedroom. Starve him. Wait for his abduction to come on the news so Cooper could find out where the mother lived and send a ransom note. She smiled at the scenario, having fun visualising how thin the kid would get, his ribs showing from beneath his skin.

Finally, the mother glanced in Kayla's direction. The boy was two meters away from Kayla, eyeing up her brownie packet, and if his mum wasn't looking, Kayla would have pulled a nasty face at him to make him cry.

"Caleb! Come back here."

Kayla got up, kicked the ball towards him, annoyed it hadn't whacked him in the gut, then walked to the main gates, popping her rubbish in the overflowing bin. Needing to be spiteful, the urge never far away, she went to the bench where the bloke slept and swept his feet to the ground.

The rest of him fell off, and he gazed up at her, blinking. "What did you do *that* for?"

She stared at him. "Other people want to sit here as well, you know. You can't hog the whole seat." She plonked herself down and crossed her legs, placing her bag next to her so there wasn't much room for him if he chose to sit near her.

"Arsehole," he muttered.

She thought about booting him in the face. "Homeless prick."

"I'm not homeless. I sleep in the shelter."

"Still homeless. Still a waste of space who gets kicked out every morning until night-time. I bet you're on benefits. Scum, that's what you are."

He manoeuvred to his feet. Swayed. "You could do with learning some humility."

"And you could learn to have a fucking shower. You stink." She stood. Picked up her bag.

He shook his head. "Got any spare change?"

She laughed. He could take a running jump if he thought she'd dip her hand in her purse. "Get a job." She walked off, stopping by the drug seller at the gate. "How much is a wrap?"

He looked her up and down. "Dunno what you're on about."

"Yes you do. How much?"

He told her. She nodded, filing that information away. She'd tell Cooper later, and he could sell his gear a bit cheaper, undercut all the pushers around here. It was a good job he didn't sell anywhere near Roach's patches, else there'd be trouble.

Maybe he should ask Everett if he can work for his 'mate'.

At least then Cooper wouldn't risk getting caught. As Everett, he knew Cooper sold drugs, they'd admitted that was why they'd been kicked out of that house, so why hadn't he done something about it as Roach?

She trotted back to work, pausing outside to send Cooper a message.

Kayla: Text Everett. Say you don't want to step on his mate's toes by selling drugs. Ask if the mate's got an opening so you can work for him/Roach.

Cooper: Why, have you got a bad feeling?

Kayla: Yeah, just do it.

Then she texted Everett.

Kayla: It's a go with Alice.

Everett: Good girl.

She entered the office building, pleased with herself.

The receptionist raised her eyebrows. "Someone looks like the cat that got the cream."

I'll have more than that if I play my cards right. "It's a nice day. The sun always brings out the best in me."

She returned to her desk, looking forward to Alice's death day tomorrow.

Chapter Three

In the hallway, Everett watched through the gap by the hinges, staring into the living room and hoping they didn't see him. Dad glared at Mum, his face red, weird purple worms standing out beside his eyes near his hairline. The worms bulged when he was angry, and Everett had to wait for them to disappear before he dared speak to him. But he wanted to speak now, he wanted to stick up for Mum who wiped tears from her cheeks and hiccupped because she'd cried so much. Dad's slaps hurt. His hand must be made of metal or something.

Don't speak. Don't speak. Don't speak.

"What have I told you?" Dad said. "What the fucking fuck have I told you, Helen?"

"I'm sorry, Shaun."

"You're always sorry—afterwards—and you didn't answer my question."

"I mustn't talk back."

"Right. And what did you do?"

"I talked back."

"And what happens when you talk back?"

"You hit me."

"That's correct, so why do you keep doing it?"

"I don't know."

Everett knew. If Mum was the same as him, every time he got slapped or punched, he wanted to shout at Dad and tell him to piss off. He'd get walloped for swearing then, but the urge was so strong he had to bite his tongue to stop himself. Mrs Watson at school said parents hitting their children was wrong, but in the playground, loads of kids said they got smacked. Dad said he could hit Everett and Mum all he bloody well liked, thank you very much, and no one could tell him otherwise. When they were alone, Dad off to the Green Dragon, Mum said they shouldn't be hit either but it was best to just let him get on with it else he'd get worse. It was confusing, being taught different opinions. Which one was he supposed to believe? Which one was less likely to get him punished?

"I'm going out," Dad said, "and that dinner had better be on the table when I get back at five."

Everett tiptoed to the kitchen and hid beside the fridge in the dining room side. He listened: the rustle of Dad putting his shoes on; the click of the handle going down; the slam of the front door.

"Everett?" Mum called.

He darted out from his hiding place, running to meet her halfway down the hallway. She held her arms out to him, and he hugged her, his face squashed against her flat belly. Her hip bone dug into his arm; Dad said slags only deserved to eat like sparrows and 'fat' women were a turn-off.

What was a turn-off?

"Did you see everything?" she asked, rubbing the top of his head.

"Yeah."

"You know you should stay upstairs when he starts."

"But..."

"Do as you're told, okay? I don't want you getting caught in the crossfire."

He'd asked her once what that word meant, and she'd explained. From then on, he'd imagined bullets flying instead of fists and one of them hitting him instead. Dad wouldn't care if it did, he'd say Everett should have minded his own business. Then again, he'd likely say his son could learn a thing or two from him and make him sit on the sofa to watch.

Sometimes, Dad hit Mum in the bedroom, then this squeaking sound came, Mum crying, Dad making weird noises. She'd screamed last week, asking him to stop, and a slap had shut her up. The next day, she'd had a split lip.

"Can I help you make dinner?" He looked up at her, praying she'd say yes. If she did, it meant it would be on the table on time and she wouldn't get told off.

"Okay. You're such a good boy."

He made the crumble topping for pudding—Dad loved apple crumble and custard, and Mum usually made it if she'd really upset him. Everett liked the feeling of the squidgy butter on his fingers when he mixed it with flour and sugar. She peeled the apples and let him eat the red skin while she browned mince for shepherd's pie. He laid most of the apple pieces in the glass dish, leaving some for her to make the apple sauce.

He loved afternoons like this, just him and her, but they were always ruined by thoughts of Dad getting drunk on beer and coming home to pick on them again. He wished he had a different dad, one who played football with him down the park and stuff like that. Boycie's dad did that, even though he was a meanie head, and sometimes they went to proper Spurs games. Most of the time, though, they watched the local pub team Dad said was shit.

With the pie and crumble in the oven, Mum showed Everett how to make lemonade. It'd be fizzy later by using next door's SodaStream—Vi's husband got loads of things off the back of a lorry, and she said Mum could use them whenever she wanted. Everett liked the toasted sandwich maker the best.

Time passed too quickly, and the thud of Dad's footsteps up the garden path had Everett and Mum quickly checking if they'd tidied everything up. She whipped to the oven to get the dinner onto the table, placing all the dishes on wicker mats. She stirred the custard on the hob, then turned the gas off so it could cool and form a skin. Dad liked the skin, especially because she sprinkled sugar on top and it melted.

Dad entered the kitchen, staring at the table and nodding. He sat, and Everett got the plates out, anxious he might drop one and smash it. He'd be in for it then. But he managed, even under Dad's watchful stare, then he collected the knives and forks.

Mum poured gravy into a jug. They sat and ate, Dad shovelling it in, his plate so full the food threatened to fall off the edge. Mum only had enough to cover the middle of hers, the same amount as Everett.

"I've just heard Boycie's dad's got the same problem I have," Dad said with his mouth full. "That fucking bitch wife of his…he had to clout her today an' all. I don't get where you women's manners have gone. It's all this equality bullshit that's the problem. You think you should be treated the same as us. Fucking liberty."

Boycie got smacked by his dad, too. At playtime in school, they talked about how much their bums and the backs of their legs hurt. Once, Boycie had a bruise on his thigh where he'd been hit with the end of a golf club. His mum thought the bone had broken, but she was too scared to take him to the doctor. He'd limped for ages after.

Dad cleared his plate and went for seconds. Mum ate slowly—she said if she did that, her tummy thought it was fuller than it was. Everett had asked her once why she didn't eat a sandwich when Dad wasn't looking, but she reckoned he'd know because she'd put on weight.

One day, she'd said, they'd run away.
Everett couldn't wait.

Chapter Four

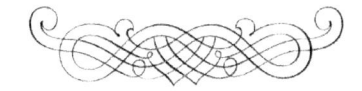

Alice sat at one of the tables in the kitchen at Haven, thinking about her friend's kind gesture. Vicky was one of those people who was nasty on the outside but soft inside. She'd had to grow a hard outer shell because of Parker, who'd treated her like shit. That time when he'd breached Haven's wall, jumping over and getting onto the grounds, God, it had been frightening. He'd found out where Vicky was, obviously, and it meant the twins had now posted more security guards around the perimeter, not just at the front.

Vicky had left Haven shortly after. She hadn't felt safe anymore, which was understandable, and anyway, she planned to kill Parker. Being at Haven prevented that, what with their movements being monitored in order to keep them safe. Alice just hoped Vicky wouldn't get caught.

Did Parker deserve to die? She struggled with that line of thinking. It wasn't right. She shouldn't be entertaining thoughts like that, but as she'd learned from seeing the twins' therapist, the mind of the abused was a troubled place, and if your abuser was dead, it was easier to move on. No fear left, see. How many times had she said that to herself about Everett? "If he could just die, everything would be all right. If he wasn't here, I wouldn't have to worry anymore." She was coming to terms with it being a natural response to trauma, but it didn't mean she had to like it.

George and Greg had asked her where Everett lived, his daily patterns, and she'd been surprised she didn't have many concrete answers. Of course she knew where he lived, she'd lived there, too, but as for what he did during the day for a living, she had no idea. All he'd ever said was he was a businessman with his best friend, Boycie. She didn't know his real name. Why hadn't she asked where they worked? Why hadn't she prodded them for specifics about what they actually did? Why had she let Everett skate over that information as if it didn't matter? Maybe, and she hated to admit this, at the time she'd just been grateful to have a man who'd insisted on paying all the bills, and he'd come across as modest, not wanting to brag about himself.

Until he'd changed and hit her.

She hadn't wanted to stay once he'd shown her he *wasn't* sorry after the first few times he'd punched her, plus the gaslighting, where he turned it round to say *she'd* hit *him*. She'd given him several chances, and when it kept happening, her friends telling her to run, she'd run. But he'd found her, and she could kick herself now for opening the door to him every night in that flat, like she'd *wanted* to be punched. She'd thought that by talking to him he'd see her point of view eventually—how naïve was *that*?

He'd made out, each visit, that he was prepared to listen, then he'd turned nasty on her. Maybe she'd still been in a certain mindset, wanting to fix things, for them to be the couple they used to be.

Thankful she'd heard about Haven, she'd come here with the sole purpose of getting her head on straight and thinking about leaving London. Changing her name maybe, being a whole new person.

With Vicky gone, and much as she'd appreciated her friendship, Alice could think clearer without her influence. Vicky meant well, and she seemed to have clung on to Alice as a lifeline, wanting Everett to die as much as she did Parker. But Alice wasn't a killer. She didn't have it in her, no matter how many times she'd wished her ex-husband dead. Without Vicky going on in her ear, she'd been able to concentrate on what mattered to her—healing while at Haven then, when she was strong enough, getting away.

She was almost there emotionally. Despite what Everett had done to her, for the first few weeks she'd justified it, blaming herself, which was what these types of abusers did, convincing you it was your fault. She saw herself in every new woman who walked through Haven's doors, sometimes wincing at how pathetic she'd been, holding on to a romanticised version of her life that wasn't even close to the truth. Yes, those early days with Everett had been good, but she now understood she'd been love bombed, swept off her feet. She'd been groomed and manipulated to behave how he'd wanted, and for a while, oblivious, she'd complied.

Until she hadn't.

The only people she'd told about the abuse were her two friends and the people at Haven. Shame meant she'd kept it from family, not wanting them to hurt along with her. Besides, would they even believe Everett had hit her when he was so good at convincing Alice that she'd hit him instead? Bloody hell, now she looked back on it, how he was able to sway her into thinking *she* was the abuser…it just went to show how deep gaslighting went, how it could make you believe one thing when you knew it wasn't the truth. Twice he'd done that, making out his attacks hadn't happened, and twice she'd wondered if she'd imagined it.

He'd really fucked with her.

She sighed. Pulled herself out of her head and back into the room. The new cook, Edna, must be about seventy if she was a day, a robust type who bustled about. Every so often she swigged from a silver hip flask kept in her apron pocket, then continued with her job. She had weird skin, her cheeks with a matte look to them, and they never went red from where she stood in front of the hot cooker.

Alice had to give it to her, she made the best cakes, and her stews weren't half bad either. But she wasn't the kind and caring Lucia, and Alice found it difficult to warm to the new woman. The twins thought she was the bee's knees, but then Edna behaved differently when they were around. If Alice didn't know better, she'd say Edna didn't like the women staying at Haven.

Two ladies played cards at a nearby table, their kids having a nap. Alice sent up a silent prayer of thanks that she'd never had children with Everett. God, she'd have been tied to him for life then, and he'd more than likely have put in for full custody, making up some bullshit that she was a bad mother.

Why had he turned so nasty? Was it to do with his childhood? The therapist had asked her that, and she'd been unable to answer. Everett hadn't gone into any detail other than his mum had left when he was small and he no longer spoke to his dad. She hadn't pushed, sensing it was too painful for him to talk about, but now she wished she'd poked the bear, found out what gave him the idea he could treat her like shit.

She had yet to decide what she wanted the twins to do regarding him. Scare him or beat him up? Or neither of those things. The only worry she had was that he'd find another poor cow to pick on, and if she didn't let George and Greg warn Everett about ever hitting a woman again, then someone else would go through what she had.

Edna plonked a large tray of toasted sandwiches on an empty table. She returned to the worktop to collect cheese scones and two blocks of butter and all but dropped them beside the sandwiches. She peered at Alice, a manic glint in her eye. What was the matter with her?

"You need to eat more," Edna said. "You're a skinny mare, aren't you."

"She's not a mare," Tricia, one of the other women, said. "And maybe she's too nervous to eat much. I know the feeling."

Alice smiled at Tricia, and Olivia, the newest lady. "The things men do to us, eh?"

"The things you *let* them do." Edna tromped off to clean up the worktop.

Olivia gawped at the cook's back. "You what?"

Edna turned. "You all need to grow a backbone, stop letting people walk all over you. How can you expect sympathy when you've brought it all on yourself? I'd have walked after the first punch, I wouldn't hang around for more. Take you for instance, Alice. Why the hell did you open that front door, night after night, when you admitted you'd seen it was your ex through the peephole? Do you have *any* brain cells?"

Alice caught sight of Sharon standing in the kitchen doorway. She ran Haven and had empathy for miles.

"Did I just hear right, Edna?"

The old woman turned to Sharon. Edna looked like she wanted to kick herself, her eyes darting about but her face expressionless. Come to think of it, she never had an expression, her features always blank. It gave Alice the willies.

Edna sniffed and seemed to be mentally telling herself off. "I say it like it is."

Sharon narrowed her eyes. "I'll be telling the twins about this. I can guarantee they won't want you saying nasty shit like that. You can have opinions, just keep them to yourself here, all right? You're a cook not a therapist—and if you *were* a therapist, I wouldn't want to come and see you. Christ."

Edna shrugged. "It's just I've never got why women put up with it all. Can't get my head around it."

"Not everyone's strong," Sharon said. "And these sorts of abusers, they have ways of getting inside your head. Be grateful you've never been through it." She pressed a button beside the doorframe that let off a quiet buzz in all the rooms to inform the others lunch was ready. She took a stack of plates from the sideboard and placed it beside the sandwiches. "Are you okay, Alice?"

A quick nod, and Alice reached for a sandwich. "I don't like her," she whispered.

"I'm beginning to think the twins made a mistake," Sharon whispered back.

"I'm not deaf," Edna snapped. "And you've got it wrong. *I* made a mistake coming here. I'll collect my bag and be on my way. This place was screwing with my head anyway."

Lucia used to live in, but Edna had a bungalow she wasn't prepared to give up. Just as well, really, if she was throwing in the towel. She walked out, and Sharon stared after her.

"Thank fuck for that," Tricia said. "Good food, bad attitude. I didn't like the way she kept staring at me like I was shit on her shoe."

"Glad it wasn't just me." Alice sighed.

The front door slammed.

Sharon picked up a sandwich. "Anyone good at cooking?"

Olivia laughed. "Edna's already sorted dinner. There's five slow cookers on the go in the utility room. Chilli. We'll just have to make the rice. We'll manage between us."

Sharon took her phone out of her pocket. "I'd better let the twins know. They might want to have a word with her, you know, remind her that what goes on here is a secret." She wandered out.

Other women filed in, and Alice ate her sandwich. She needed to speak to Sharon about going out for the morning tomorrow. Vicky must be back at work if she could afford to pay for a haircut and nails. Where was she living now? Had she seen Parker since the day he'd vaulted the wall? Alice had asked in messages, but Vicky had said she didn't want to talk about him. Odd, when that was *all* she'd talked about at Haven. Maybe she was being kind, not going into detail about the man so if the police checked Vicky's messages when he was dead, Alice couldn't be accused of being involved.

She worried about that. Being asked questions. She'd have to lie and say Vicky hadn't spoken to her about killing Parker, but would the other women here do the same? Vicky had been so vocal about it. But maybe that had been bravado and she didn't plan to kill him at all but had just bigged herself up so she looked tough.

Alice finished her sandwich and buttered a scone. She tuned out the chatter around her and thought about tomorrow. How would she feel if she saw Everett? She was stronger now, but there was still a nugget or two of fear inside her. Would she go cold all over? Run?

Don't be daft. Unless he's found out where I am, how will he even know where I've gone, where to look?

She ate the last of her scone and left the room to find Sharon in her office. A tap on the door didn't yield a response, and Alice frowned. Tapped again.

"Who is it?"

"Alice."

"Come in."

Alice stepped inside. Sharon sat at her desk, elbows propped on it, her face in her hands. She lowered them, folding her arms.

"Are you okay?" Alice shut the door and sat.

"Tired. Two cooks, gone in a short space of time. George isn't happy about the way Edna spoke to you three. They're going to have a word with her."

"Oh God."

"Not your problem. She lied to us in her interview, said she had empathy. Clearly not." Sharon smiled, an obvious attempt at trying to brighten up. "What can I do for you?"

"Vicky messaged to ask if I could go to the hairdresser with her tomorrow."

"What for when Stacey comes here once a week?"

Alice shrugged. "She mentioned me having my nails done, too. She's paying. I said I'd go— it's at Curls and Tongs. Vicky's picking me up in a taxi at ten."

"Are you sure you want to be out with her, considering Parker's such an arsehole? What if he's following her around? We don't know what's been going on with her since she left; she seems to have dropped off the face of the earth. She won't answer any of the messages I sent her on the phone she was given when she came here. You'll be careful, won't you? Any sign of trouble, you'll ring the twins?"

"Can you get hold of them and let them know that's where I'm going? Maybe they'll nip there while I'm having my hair done. Keep an eye out."

Sharon nodded. "They might insist on dropping you off or at least following your taxi. Do you know how long you'll be? Just so I can make a note of it, then if you're not back when you say you will be…"

Alice smiled. "I have no idea. I'll message Vicky and ask, then let you know."

Chapter Five

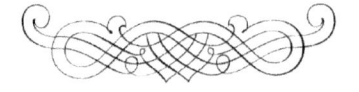

The twins' taxi sped along the street, Greg gritting his teeth, the muscle in his jaw spasming. George, glad he wasn't the only arsey one, took a lemon sherbet out of the glove box and unwrapped it. He thought about what Edna had said to three of the women. She obviously didn't understand the intricacies of abusive relationships, and he was glad she'd never suffered, but when working with victims, her brand of snark wasn't welcome. Making women feel like they were at fault went against everything they were trying to do at Haven.

"I'm full-on fucking raging." He shoved the sweet in his mouth and crunched on it to give him something to focus on other than the fury swirling inside him. He hated making mistakes and could have sworn the old dear was the right woman for the cook's job. While it was a bit weird, her face never betraying her feelings, he'd put that down to her being old and learning to school her features.

Her change of heart regarding the women had pissed him off. During her interview, she'd expressed sorrow for anyone in a domestic violence relationship, her eyes watering at one point. Why the change of heart? Had she been lying to get the position? He could understand her not wanting to go all in like Lucia and live at Haven, what with Edna having her own bungalow, but she'd been over-the-top adamant that she'd stick to her hours and wouldn't do overtime. While that wasn't odd, it bothered him now. Did she have someone at home she needed to be there for and she'd lied about that, too?

Now George had started thinking about it, his mind threw up all sorts. He questioned their eagerness to take her on, possibly because having no cook presented a problem in how to feed all the women and their kids. Had they been so desperate to fill Lucia's position that they hadn't looked into Edna as much as they should?

Why would anyone who thought abused women needed to grow a backbone want to work at a fucking refuge? Why had she told Sharon 'I say it like it is' when she hadn't before? And why couldn't she get her head around women taking abuse when, in her interview, she'd had all the sympathy in the world and had seemed to understand the ins and outs perfectly?

It's like she's two different people.

"She lied to us," Greg said, taking a left onto the housing estate where Edna lived. "Outright conned us to get the job. If she wasn't so fucking old…"

"What, you'd do her over?"

"Yeah."

"What was it you said to me about women and how they should take their punishment like everyone else? So are you saying that doesn't apply because she's got wrinkles and grey hair?" George asked.

"Seems a bit much, granny bashing."

"If it was a bloke, you'd slap him about a bit."

"True. Let's just see what she has to say for herself before we make any decisions."

George cleared his throat. "Whatever. I don't like the fact she said stuff to the women. It could set their recovery back, all that hard work in therapy going down the shitter. I could strangle the silly bitch."

"Best you do that in private, eh?"

"Why say that? Of course she'd be taken to the warehouse or the cottage. Jesus."

"It's just I know what you're like when it comes to women suffering like Mum. You'll want to give Edna a whack as soon as you see her."

"I've got *some* restraint, bruv."

Greg parked outside Edna's bungalow. "She keeps the garden nice."

"Or that woman just there does." George pointed to a slim blonde on her knees planting flowers. Long-sleeved T-shirt. Jeans. A bandana tied around her neck. Gardening gloves. "Might be her granddaughter or something." He got out and waited for Greg, then led the way up the garden path.

The woman looked up at them, sunglasses shielding her eyes, the peak of her red baseball cap casting a shadow over her cheeks and nose. "Um, can I help you?"

George flashed her a smile. "Is Edna back from work yet?"

She put down a plastic pot with pink flowers in it. "I don't work."

George needed a second to process that. "*You're* Edna?"

"Yes..."

"So who's the old bird who lives here?"

She frowned. "There isn't one. Only I live here..." She stood and dusted off her gloves, small bits of mud falling off. "And thanks for assuming I'd be old just because of my name. Happens every single time, so I don't know why I'm surprised. What's going on?"

George scratched his forehead. "Err, I don't actually know. We employed a lady called Edna Wiggins who gave this address as hers. She's in her eighties."

"Well, that's definitely not me." She gestured to herself and laughed. "Unless I've aged since I got up this morning."

"Are you fucking us about?" Greg asked. "Are you pretending to be Edna and she's inside?"

"Why the hell would I do that? This is my property, I've lived here for ten years. My nan left it to me in her will."

"Do you know who we are?" George asked, feeling like an egotistical prick for saying that, one of those famous knobs who thought everyone in the world should recognise them.

"I've worked it out, seeing as you're twins." She knelt again as if bored by them. "I don't know what you want me to say. Ask around about me if you like." She wafted an arm at the street. "I'm sure her over the road will tell you what day I moved in and the specific time. She watched it all going on. Oh, and I do have an elderly visitor sometimes, my nan's mate, so Nosy Beak is sure to tell you about her an' all."

"Right." George shoved his hands in his pockets. "Well, cheers for your time. Nice garden." He walked off and got in the taxi. Once Greg had joined him, he said, "What the actual fuck?"

"Hmm. Why would an old lady lie about where she lives and, so it seems, steal someone else's name? In future, our checks need to be more thorough. All we did was make sure an Edna lived there, we didn't send anyone out to watch her for a bit before we employed her, so who is she really?"

George pinched the bridge of his nose. "God knows, but all the women at the refuge could be compromised if she wasn't there to just cook food."

Greg drove off. "Fuck."

George and Greg stood in the CCTV office with Bennett, one of their men. His colleague wasn't in today, and George was glad about that. The bloke was a bit of a scaredy-cat and got on his tits.

Bennett sat at his computer, ready to search for what they needed. George gave Old Edna's description and the Haven address, requesting any footage from around that area showing an elderly lady heading in the direction of the bungalow.

"Is that her?" Bennett paused the recording taken around ten minutes after Edna had left the refuge.

"Yeah. Press play," George said.

Edna, or whoever the fuck she was, walked past a row of shops on the housing estate closest to Haven. She popped into a newsagent's and reemerged with a carrier bag that appeared half full. She continued past the kebab place and went around a corner at the end of the parade. Bennett switched cameras and found the footage of the road she'd turned onto. She appeared, stopping to lean on a wall and possibly get her breath back. It *was* hot, so he could understand an old dear needing to pause. She trotted along until she came to an alley and disappeared down it.

"That's your lot," Bennett said. "I can tell you for a fact there aren't any more cameras between there and the address you gave me. She's in the wind, mate. Why are you after a granny anyway?"

"Because she gave us a fake name. We've just been to what we thought was her bungalow, but someone else lives there. And before you say it, yes, we'll have her checked out."

"I wasn't about to teach you to suck eggs." Bennett clicked the screens off.

George handed him an envelope. "If you happen to see the oldie again, give us a bell."

"Will do."

They left the office, George miffed that the footage had basically shown them fuck all that was any good to them. "Do you reckon she wanted cash in hand as her wages for a reason?"

Greg nodded as they got into the taxi. "Seems like it."

George put his seat belt on. "I'm really uneasy about why she was at Haven. Why she had to be there, then leave as abruptly as she did. Had she done what she needed to so it didn't matter if she jacked her job in?"

"People who give false names and addresses aren't exactly on the level, are they, so she was up to something. We've upped security, so if Old Edna was scoping Haven out, she'll know trying to break in is pointless."

"We should go back and talk to Nosy Beak over the road from that bungalow, see if she's noticed anything. Young Edna said her nan's mate visits her, but what if that's a lie? Or what if the mate is our Edna and she's pinched that name and address? Maybe the neighbour can describe the old girl to us, and if she matches our cook, then we've got a bit more to go on."

How could they find an old woman in a haystack, though?

***

Maud Stokes wasn't as nosy as Young Edna had made out. She sat in a chair at the back of her living room which faced the street. Nets didn't hide the view. Young Edna was easy enough to see, gardening her heart out.

"I don't keep watch out there anymore," Maud said. "Not like I used to. I ran the Neighbourhood Watch scheme along here, but it all got too much. I stepped back from getting involved with anyone because it only brings trouble."

"So you haven't noticed an older lady visiting Edna, then?"

"I tend to stay away from her over the road. I don't go out if she's around. She's…well, she isn't right. I had an altercation with her a couple of years ago where she accused me of spying on her when I was doing no such thing. I was actually washing the inside of my windows, and she came storming over, shouting the odds. She's on drugs, I reckon. She was jittery and manic, paranoid."

Through the window, George looked to where Young Edna was. "You must have noticed how often she's in her garden, surely. You've got a prime spot in that chair, and movement out there must catch your attention."

"Well, yes, but... I saw you speaking to her earlier, and now you're here, she might come across and accuse me of something again, and I really don't want that."

"We'll have a word with her in a sec. So is she in her garden often? She must be, considering how neat it is."

"Not much the past few months, it's been raining a lot, but since the weather turned nice, she's been out there every evening."

Sensing Maud wasn't going to be of any further help, George jerked his head at Greg. They were wasting their time here. "We'll leave you be, then." He took an envelope containing fifty quid from his pocket and dropped it on her side table.

"I'll not become one of your grasses," Maud said.

You wouldn't be much cop if you were.

Back outside, George led the way across the street.

Edna stood from her crouch at a flowerbed and sighed. "What did she have to say for herself?"

George stared at her, wishing he could see her eyes. It annoyed him, speaking to people who had sunglasses on. "Nothing much, other than you had a go at her a while back. Don't do that again, eh? If we find out you've gone and bothered her, we'll be back."

"She pissed me off, that's all. Got a petition going with the Neighbourhood Watch freaks to get rid of me. I went over and told her to back off, end of story. The main reason they wanted me gone was because they think I'm weird, whatever that means."

George shook his head. "Just remember what I said, all right?"

She nodded. "Your wish is my command." She laughed, and it made her sound deranged.

George glanced at Greg: *What the fuck?* Was it drugs, like Maud had said? He studied her, the twitch of her mouth. Yeah, she was on something. Or maybe coming down off it.

"Are you tweaking?" he asked.

"Ah, so she's told you about me supposedly being on drugs, has she? Honestly, she's a troublemaker, or she used to be. Take what she says with a pinch of salt."

Leaving her to it, they got back in the taxi.

"Sounds like the usual neighbour dispute bullshit to me." Greg peeled away from the kerb. "Maud was a busybody, and Edna called her out on it."

George took two sweets out and opened one for Greg, putting it in his brother's mouth. "Eat that. I need to shut you up while I have a think."

"We'll get to the bottom of this eventually."

George nodded but wasn't so sure. "What part of shutting up didn't you understand?"

"Fucking hell, keep your hair on."

George ignored him and had that think, determined to find Old Edna and see what the hell was going on.

Chapter Six

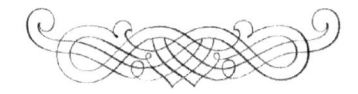

Sweating in her long-sleeved top, Edna watched the taxi drive away and prayed the twins wouldn't call her bluff and poke into who she was. It wouldn't take long for the other nosy neighbours to blab that Roach had visited a few times when he'd discussed her role at Haven. She was surprised Maud hadn't spotted that, but maybe Edna giving her a scare meant the silly old cow didn't want to pass anything on to the twins.

The disguise Roach had provided for her at Haven had been uncomfortable—it needed glue at the neck and on her chest to hold the old-lady prosthetic face in place, and on the forearms for the wrinkled hands that were creepy, second-skin gloves, complete with nails. As for the grey-haired wig, it had itched. The body suit was the worst, heavy and cumbersome, giving her a pot belly, big boobs, and thick thighs. Still, she didn't have to go back there now, her shenanigans this morning giving her the opportunity for a hasty exit. Roach didn't need her there anymore, his ex was getting killed tomorrow, so he'd told her to get the hell out. Thank God she'd had a mood slump where she'd expressed her true views. It had given her the perfect escape.

She'd come home, shed her disguise, and put on clothing that hid the glue residue so she could do some gardening as quickly as possible. Her mind needed stabilising, she'd had a bit of an episode at Haven with the way she'd behaved, and the only way she'd found to calm herself was to dive into something she could concentrate on.

She'd questioned Roach's methods, using her real name and address, but he reckoned it'd be okay. He'd sent some woman called Kayla into the refuge using someone else's name, so why hadn't he done the same with Edna? Still, the twins had appeared sufficiently confused and hopefully thought someone had stolen Edna's identity. As long as they didn't come back, she could resume her life. Gardening, pottering around her place, earning money from filling out online questionnaires, something she'd done obsessively before her stint at Haven in order to cope with her manic episodes and draw her out of the depressive ones. She had the cash-in-hand wages she'd insisted on from Haven plus the wedge she'd received from Roach, her former dealer.

He'd offered to pay her in drugs, but she wasn't an addict now. She'd gone cold turkey to get herself off the cocaine, and the questionnaires had been her lifeline during a time of pure hell from not taking her bipolar meds, something to focus on other than the gnawing need for respite and oblivion that had tried to eat her alive. Her Personal Independence Payment benefits sorted the bills, housing benefit the rent. She gave her medication to Roach in exchange for money for food. That was part of what he did; people pretended to be depressed so they were given tablets. He bought them, sold them on. The cash flowed.

Finally feeling some semblance of normality despite the twins' visit, she went inside, stripping off her gloves, the bandana, which had stuck to her throat, and her top. Glad of the cool air from the fans drying up the sweat, she picked up her phone.

EDNA: I'M OUT OF HAVEN. POSSIBLE PROBLEM. THE TWINS CAME TO SEE ME AT HOME. THEY KNOW I'M THE REAL EDNA. PROBABLY LOOKING FOR THE OLD ONE NOW.

ROACH: IF THEY COME BACK, FOB THEM OFF LEAVE THE DISGUISE IN YOUR BACK GARDEN. SOMEONE WILL COME TO COLLECT IT IN THE NIGHT.

EDNA: OKAY.

First, she washed the glue off her neck and arms using the lotion Roach had provided. Bagged up the disguise and tied up the black bag handles, popping it outside. She had a shower, and the relief of the shampoo easing away the itch on her scalp was heaven. She fancied a late lunch out so got ready. Maybe she'd get lucky and find a willing bloke if she stayed in the pub until this evening. She always went back to their place, hers too messy and disorganised for her to want anyone to see it.

Her walk to the Noodle coated her body in sweat again, the sun relentless. She entered, glad of the air-conditioning, and ordered a baguette and Coke. The place was busy, and she settled at a table for two in the corner. Free of her Haven responsibilities, she allowed herself to relax. To think about her dream of opening a cake shop. Those abused women had raved about her baking. But how would she go about getting a lease, and wouldn't she need qualifications in cooking to be able to sell her produce? She'd need certificates. Maybe Roach would advise her on that. If he helped her out with start-up cash, he might take a cut of the profits so she could pay him back. What he'd asked her to do, playing a part in his ex's murder, well, he owed her, didn't he?

With something to look forward which would keep her mind on track, she ate her food and dreamed of a better life. Maybe, because she'd done Roach that huge favour of being a cook at Haven so she could spy on Alice, he'd stop taking her medication from her if she asked. She really ought to get back on it. Trying to control her illness without drugs had been harder than ever lately, the lows sending her to the depths of depression, her bed becoming her best friend. And when she was manic, it was more severe — she barely knew what to do with the excess energy and her spiralling thoughts.

She messaged Roach.

EDNA: ANY CHANCE I CAN STOP SELLING MY MEDS FOR A BIT?

ROACH: YEAH.

She had a new prescription waiting at the chemist. She'd go there after she'd drunk her Coke, pop a pill, then come back. It'd take her a couple of weeks to get used to the lithium in her system again, but she'd done it before, knew how to deal with it. It stabilised her moods, and she looked forward to feeling okay again, to not monitoring her self-care, the ups and downs, which was exhausting.

A burden had been lifted. No more meeting up with Roach to hand over the tablets. No more needing the money. And if Roach would help her start a business, even if it was a market stall, she'd never have to sell her lifeline to him again.

Chapter Seven

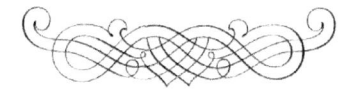

The day had come for them to run. Everett went to school, as usual. Mum would pick him up later with their suitcase, and they'd go to the train station. They were going to South Shields where Granny and Grampy lived by the sea. They had a holiday there every summer, the only time Dad wasn't with them. Everett always walked to the beach with Grampy and

Mum stayed behind and talked to Granny about life, whatever that meant. Mum had phoned her last week when Dad was at the Green Dragon, and they'd made the final plans to leave. Mum would work in the factory up there, and they'd live in a little house down the road from the Co-op.

He couldn't wait for the end of the school day. He'd miss Boycie and Precious, but he could write to them, Mum said, only he couldn't let them know where they'd gone. He'd almost blabbed they were running away but stopped himself in time, remembering what Mum had told him: if Dad knew what they were up to, he'd stop them, make them stay.

Throughout story time, sitting on the carpet, he imagined splashing in the sea at the weekend and learning to swim in the big pool in the sports centre round the corner from Granny's. Grampy was going to teach him every Saturday morning, then they'd go off to the beach for a picnic while Mum used the washing machine at Granny's because their new house didn't have one yet. Mum said it would take time for her to afford everything they needed, but she'd get there.

Mrs Watson finished the story and closed the book. "Please go and get your coats and shoes on, and have a lovely weekend. I'll see you on Monday."

Everyone scrambled up and rushed to the cloakroom, Everett pushing people out of the way he was that excited to get out. He switched his plimsolls for his shoes and stuffed his arms in his coat pockets, doing up the zip, the first in line at the door. He stared out into the playground, looking for Mum but couldn't see her. Too many other mums stood in a huddle.

Mrs Watson opened the door and, as usual, held her hand out to stop the kids from running off. They weren't allowed to go unless their parents were there. Everett had to step to the side and let Boycie go first, then other children, then Precious, until Everett was the only one left. All the mummies and a couple of dads had gone.

"Let's go to reception and ring Mummy, shall we?"

Everett's tummy hurt. What if Mum had been caught packing the suitcase? Dad was working in Ilford today, and he always got home late on those days because of the traffic, so it couldn't be him. None of the neighbours would have seen her leaving the house either, as they all went to work. He imagined the taxi driver knowing Dad and phoning him in secret.

Mrs Watson asked the secretary to look up Everett's number, then she dialled. She seemed to stand there for ages with the phone to her ear, and Everett felt sick.

"Oh, there's no answer, so maybe she's on her way here. We'll go back to the cloakroom door, all right?"

Everett followed her there, his stomach hurting even more, especially when he spotted Dad standing in the playground all by himself.

"Oh, Daddy's here." Mrs Watson opened the door.

She ushered Everett out, and he wanted to tell her about home, that Dad hit him and Mum, that he shouted and the worms came. But he didn't. Dad smiled, and Everett stepped forward. He trailed Dad out of the playground and onto the pavement that led to their house. They walked two streets before Everett had the guts to speak.

"Where's Mum?" He glanced up at him.

"She didn't make it. Got herself hurt."

That usually meant Dad had hit her. He always blamed her, as if she'd hurt herself, when it was him who'd done it. Same with Everett. He got slapped, and Dad would say, "Now look what you've gone and done. You made me do that."

"How did you get that bruise on your arm?" Everett asked.

"Your mother did it. Used my baseball bat on me."

Everett's whole body turned cold. Mum would be in big trouble now.

Dad turned into the garden and opened the front door. "I've got something to show you."

Everett went inside and stared at the black fabric suitcase by the bottom of the stairs. His brown teddy bear sat on top, its red bow tie skew-whiff. Mum's little handbag was next to it. So had she been at the point of leaving and Dad had come home early? Had he guessed what she was up to?

The baseball bat lay on the floor near the neat row of shoes and boots, so she must have hit him with it here. When she was just about to walk out to the taxi?

"Come with me." Dad strode down the hallway and into the kitchen.

Everett swallowed the horrible lump in his throat and went after him. Dad had gone into the garden and stood at the old outhouse which he used to store his bike and the lawnmower. There was a toilet in there an' all, although they never used it unless they were desperate when someone was using the bathroom.

Dad opened the door.

Mum sat on the loo, several holes in her forehead. They were the same size as the ones in the rabbits Dad brought home when he'd been hunting in Daffodil Woods. He used a gun with steel pellets for that, and he said a few shots were enough to kill, the gun quiet enough that no one would hear much out there amongst the trees.

No one would have heard them today either, because everyone was at work.

Blood had run in mini rivers from the holes, down Mum's face, over her nose, lips, and chin. They looked dry. Some red dots had got her white blouse dirty. She stared ahead, right at Everett, and he reckoned she was silently telling him to go and get help. But she didn't look right. Her lips were a bit blue.

"I need your help," Dad said. "She only went and fucking died, didn't she. I was aiming for her shoulder, but she moved at the last minute, so the shots went into her nut. Honestly, you couldn't make this up."

Shock and fear punched Everett in the belly. "She…she's dead?"

"Yep, and she's only got herself to blame. Did you know she was fucking off? Leaving you behind?"

Everett wouldn't tell him he'd known else he'd get a smack. He tried to process Mum being dead, that she'd never be there to save him again, but all he could think of was being stuck here with Dad. Unless Granny and Grampy came for him. He wanted to cry, to run round to Vi and tell her, but she wouldn't be back until half six. And anyway, if Dad found out he'd grassed, he'd be in so much trouble.

Hot tears itched his eyes, and he burst out crying.

"Pack that in," Dad said.

"I want my mummy…"

"Yeah, well, you can't have her. Come on, you'll be my labourer." Dad gestured to a pile of bricks he'd nicked from work for when he built a new wall out the front. They'd been sitting there for months. "You hand me the bricks while I block up the doorway. I need to take the door off first, though, then make the mortar."

Everett didn't know what that was, and he didn't care. Mum was going to be hidden behind the bricks, and Vi wouldn't even notice if she looked out of her top windows because the outhouse door didn't face the houses, it faced the row of high fir trees between this house and the one on the other side. Mr Bell wouldn't notice either. He lived alone, and his bedroom and bathroom were at the front. The back rooms were only used when his grandkids came to stay.

No one would know Mum was in there.

"We need to get a move on before she starts smelling. We've got nearly three hours before the neighbours get back."

Dad took the mower and bike out of the outhouse and stuck them in the shed. He grabbed his toolbox and got on with unscrewing the hinges, then carried the door into the shed. He filled two buckets indoors and brought them out, making the mortar on a patio slab. Everett worked out that must be the stuff that went between each brick. He stared at Mum again, wishing he could wake her up, but Dad grunted out instructions. Everett obeyed, and Dad had bricked halfway up by the time the sky grew dark. It wasn't completely night, but it was difficult to see. It meant Mum was only a dark shape.

Three-quarters had been filled.

Dad glanced at his watch and worked even faster, the whole doorway filled in, poor Mum behind it. What sort of smell did Dad mean? The whole outhouse was brick now, so would that stop the smell getting out?

"Go indoors and wash your hands. I'll tidy up out here, then we'll nip to the chippy."

For a moment, the prospect of a chippy tea erased what had happened, but then it came crashing back. Mum, dead. Everett, helping to conceal her body. Dad, a killer. Would Everett be next? Look how easy Dad had shot Mum and hidden her. Vi probably wouldn't even notice half the bricks were missing, they'd been there that long, Dad keep putting off building the wall.

Maybe Mrs Watson would help. If Everett told her on Monday, she'd know what to do, wouldn't she? He washed his hands at the kitchen sink, tears hot on his cheeks and a ball of something in his chest. It hurt, whatever it was, and fear crept inside him again, sending his arms and legs shaky. What if the police came and took Dad away? Where would Everett go then?

Dad tromped in, shut the door, and switched the light on. He snapped the curtain across the back door and came over to stand beside Everett and pull the blind down on the window. "Listen to me, kid. You tell anyone about this, and I'll kill you, *got it?"*

Everett nodded. Dad would do it, too. He never went back on his threats and promises.

"You stick to the story that she walked out on us, right? I'll get rid of the suitcase later when everyone's asleep. She had a new fella and fucked off, understand?"

Another nod.

"We'll have a proper chat over dinner, so you learn what women are really like and how they're supposed to behave. When they marry a man, they're not meant to leave them. And they're not meant to leave their little boys either. She can't have loved you if she wasn't taking you with her. Remember that when you're crying because she's not there to read you a bedtime story. She wouldn't have been there anyway because she planned to leave you with me." He ruffled Everett's

hair. "Come on. We'll get down the chippy. You can have a can of pop if you like, and a battered Mars."

It was odd, to be excited about his dinner yet at the same time a part of him was broken because Mum wouldn't be walking beside them. She must have told Dad she wasn't taking Everett with her, otherwise, how did Dad know? Everett had to face the fact she'd lied to him. He was never going to go swimming at the sports centre and have picnics on the beach.

But if that was true, why was his teddy sitting on top of the suitcase?

Chapter Eight

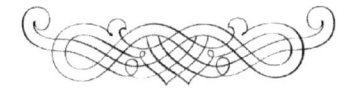

The day of the murder had dawned. Roach slapped Precious' arse. She laughed and got out of bed. He admired her naked body, all toned, like something out of a filthy men's mag, the type he'd found under Dad's bed as a kid. He gritted his teeth at his childhood intruding again but supposed it was inevitable. The past was weaved into everyone's present, the background threads still there beneath the new ones stitched on top in an attempt to hide them. Maybe he ought to take a leaf out of Boycie's book and face shit head-on instead of trying to bury it. But who wanted to dip back into a life that had been so crappy, peeling away the layers to expose the hurt?

He forced himself to think of Precious as a woman, his longtime *friend*, not a sex object in a mag. He'd play with her for a bit longer as a cover, then drop her like a sack of shit and find a new woman. She knew the score and wouldn't complain; she was used to him picking her up then letting her go. Did she ever think of him as more than a fuck buddy? Was that why she'd never had a serious relationship because she was hung up on him? It was a nice thought, having her secretly pining for him, but like he'd told himself numerous times before, they could never be a couple.

At the moment, she was a means to an end. With him being watched by the twins' men, he needed Precious as a reason why he wasn't interested in Alice or anything she did. When the police came to question him after her death, which they undoubtedly would, he could tell them he'd moved on. Precious was paid well enough to lie, to back him up.

The motorbike and helmet waited out by the communal bins, hidden beneath tarpaulin. The stolen leathers hung on the wardrobe door, the boots under her vanity unit.

She wandered out to go and have a shower. Roach swung his legs round to sit on the edge of the bed. He was meeting one of his neighbours for breakfast in the Noodle so he had an alibi for the murder. He'd chosen that pub for a reason—Nessa would clock him and confirm his presence to the twins.

As Roach, he didn't let anyone see his face, so she'd have no idea who he really was. In the Noodle he'd be Everett, the man the twins knew had thumped Alice a time or two. Yeah, they might well have a go at him about that, accuse him of killing her, but even they couldn't deny he'd sat in their own pub when she'd got shot.

Precious returned, her hair in a top knot, and slid her legs into the holes of her lacy black knickers. She popped a matching bra on. "Kayla had better come through on this and get Alice to that salon."

"She will. She hasn't let me down yet. I'm thinking of using her more often. She's played a blinder so far. I'm more bothered that Alice will back out at the last minute. Oh, and I'm going to be taking Cooper on, although he thinks my 'mate' will be his new boss, not me." Roach stood. "I'll have a quick shower then get out of your hair."

She eyed the gun on her chest of drawers. "I can't wait to get that out of my flat."

My flat, but he wasn't going to split hairs. "How did the interview go with the new tart?"

"Widow agreed with my assessment that she'll pull in a lot of punters. Young. I swear some people are born sexy."

"I'll speak to Widow and discuss whether the newbie should charge more. What's her name?"

"She goes by Goddess. Wait until you see her. You might even want to have a go with her yourself."

"Why would I do that when I've got you?"

"For now. I'm not stupid, I'm waiting to be dumped again." She gave him a filthy look, more savage than usual.

He laughed and left the room. The shower blew the cobwebs away, and he dressed in his suit and tie. Max, his neighbour, was the posh sort who'd expect Roach to scrub up well. The bloke owned a shoe factory and could talk the hind leg off a donkey about it, which was the reason Roach had chosen him. Max was so into himself he never asked Roach about his profession.

He checked Precious out. Skin-tight shorts, a fitted T-shirt. She'd wedge flip-flops and a small handbag inside her leather jacket later, ready for after the hit. "Right, remember what I said about today."

Precious rolled her eyes. "Yep, drive away, dump the bike, helmet, leathers, and boots in the specified location. Go shopping to get seen."

Roach nodded. "Good luck. Oh, and remember, I want at least three shots to her forehead, more if you can, got it?"

Precious eyed him funny. She'd never understand why he'd insisted on that, and he wasn't about to tell her. His past was none of her fucking business.

The Noodle contained someone he hadn't expected to see, and it took him a moment to remember she didn't know who he was like this—he'd always met her as Roach with his face covered. He got himself under control and strolled up to the bar, reminding himself to use the more cultured voice he adopted while being Everett. He ordered a coffee and, not seeing Max yet, went to sit at a table away from Edna.

Max came in, glanced around, and held a hand up in acknowledgement. He got a coffee and joined Roach. After a brief hello, he dived straight in, complaining about a piece of machinery in his factory that had stopped working. Production had halted for the day while an engineer sorted it out.

"I'm glad we arranged to meet," Max said. "I can't stand it when things go wrong. I'd have been no use to anyone had I stayed at work. The stress levels are unreal, and the wife can't stand me when I get flustered."

"I bet."

Max waffled some more, boring Roach's tits off.

"Shall we order breakfast then?" Roach asked. "They've got a QR code there to save us ordering at the bar now. My shout." He brought the app up on his phone and got on with it, Max yabbering on about memory foam being considered for some of his shoes. Roach let him chatter, completing the order and sitting back to drink his coffee.

"How are things with the ex now?" Max asked unexpectedly.

Since when has he been bothered about Alice? It's usually his missus who asks questions. "I've accepted she's gone and that some marriages fail. I'm seeing someone else. You know, moving on and not wallowing."

"That's good. Anyone I know?"

"I doubt it. We're keeping it low-key for now. We've both been burned in the past so want to take it slowly."

"Does Alice know?"

"I haven't seen her for a while so have no idea, and we're divorced, so it's none of her business. Her stories about me hitting her when I visited her flat became a bit tiresome, so I stopped trying to reconcile or get her to come home. I wish her nothing but the best, despite the lies she's told about me. Maybe she'll get some help for that."

"Hmm, my Isla was only talking about her this morning and how she hasn't heard from her in a while. She never told Isla anything outrageous, though, just that she'd had enough of the marriage and wanted a divorce—of course, I never told Isla what you'd had to put up with. Did you ever find out why Alice left you?"

"Nope. I gave her a nice home, a car, all those clothes, and it still wasn't enough for her. There's no pleasing some people."

"What size shoe is your new bird?"

The switch in conversation threw Roach. "No idea."

"Ask her. We've got a new line going out for autumn. I'll sort her a free pair of boots. Thigh-high ones." Max made an attempt at waggling his eyebrows. It failed.

"Thanks."

Max went into one about the new line. Roach tuned him out. Edna now chatted to a man, a beige prescription packet poking out the top of her handbag. He'd wondered how long she'd be able to stay off the lithium and coke without going off her rocker and had advised her not to sell to him for too many months in a row. She'd seen sense, at last.

He glanced at the clock behind the bar. As Max droned on, the time clicked closer to ten o'clock, and Roach smiled.

Chapter Nine

Kayla was bouncing off the walls in her Vicky disguise. She waited at the living room window so she could see the taxi coming down the long street and get out there before it stopped at the kerb.

"You're like a cat on a hot tin roof," Cooper said from his sprawled-out pose on the sofa. "Calm your tits."

"But this is so exciting. I was born to do shit like this."

"What did your boss say about you having yet another day off work?"

"Not a lot, just rolled his eyes. He clearly doesn't have any sympathy for people with depression."

"Or people making out they've got it."

Kayla laughed. "Fucking fool swallowed all my bullshit. I'm amazed at how easy it was to get the doctor to believe me an' all. I mean, he practically threw the prescription at me."

"Probably couldn't wait to get rid of you."

A motorbike shot out from behind the block of flats, Precious on her way to where she'd sit and wait down the street by Curls and Tongs. Kayla's stomach rolled over with anticipation.

"Fucking hell, Precious has just gone. It's really happening," she said.

"Of course it bloody is. Did you think someone like Roach would pull the plug once he's got something so set in his head?"

"No, but as Everett he might. And don't think of him as Roach. I'm worried you'll slip up one day and he'll twig you know who he really is."

"Fair point."

She checked the clock. "Where's that bloody taxi? I'd better go down."

"Good luck."

She left the flat, hurrying along the balcony walkway. She took the steps, not wanting to risk the lift—according to Everett, it broke down more than it worked. On the ground floor, she jogged over the grass used by the residents for kicking a ball about and picnics, and waited by the kerb. A black cab came by, a driver and a front passenger inside, and it stopped near her.

Bloody hell. Is it one of those ride shares?

The driver opened his window. "Nice to see you, Vicky."

She stared at a redheaded bloke with a beard, stunned. *Remember to speak with an Essex accent.* "What the hell's George's voice doing coming out of your mouth?"

He smiled. "We were on our way to collect Alice and happened to see you. Lucky us, eh? Get in."

Shaking from being in close proximity to the twins when she'd been helping to plan a murder, Kayla got in the back. She didn't have much choice; saying she'd wait for her own taxi might set alarm bells ringing. "Just got to cancel my Uber."

George drove away, and Kayla fired off a quick message to Everett.

KAYLA: TAXI NOT NEEDED. TWINS PICKED ME UP. EXPLAIN LATER, BUT ALL OKAY.

She turned her alert tones off.

"How have you been?" George asked. "No one's seen you about for a while."

"I've been staying with my mate."

"Who's that, then?"

"Kayla Barnes."

George tutted. "You want to watch yourself with her. She can get you in all kinds of trouble."

"Nah, she's all right. I've got a boyfriend, too, and I haven't seen Parker for yonks."

"Who's the new fella?"

Shit, I should have kept my mouth shut. "What do you need to know for?"

"We'd like to keep you safe, get him checked out," Greg said. "You worried us when you ran off like that so soon after Parker being at Haven.

We've been thinking all sorts, mainly that he caught up with you, did you a bit of damage."

"He's gone back to Essex, thank God. My cousin told me. As for the boyfriend, it isn't serious, and he's the plebby type, you know, goes to the library an' that. He'll be no trouble."

"Well, if it turns out he is, you know where to find us."

Her phone vibrated. "That's probably him now, saying good morning."

EVERETT: SHIT. HOW COME THEY KNEW YOU NEEDED A TAXI?

KAYLA: THEY DIDN'T. THEY SAW ME STANDING AT THE BLOODY KERB AND STOPPED.

EVERETT: OKAY, LET ME KNOW HOW IT GOES.

KAYLA: [THUMBS-UP EMOJI]

"Did you get yourself a job, then?" George asked. "Considering you've offered to pay for Alice to have her hair and nails done."

She'd forgotten how nosy he was. "Cash in hand, delivering leaflets. I got paid yesterday so thought I'd treat her."

"Stacey comes to Haven once a week. She'd have done Alice's hair if she'd asked."

"Yeah, but when I was there, Alice never took her up on a trim, said she felt bad at taking too much off you two as it was. Anyway, last time I saw her she needed her roots doing. She sometimes needs a nudge in the right direction, know what I mean? She got so used to Everett telling her when she could and couldn't do things that she's still in that cycle."

"He's got a new bird. Funny enough, she lives in the flats you were just at. I take it Kayla lives there an' all."

"Yeah, she moved in with her boyfriend."

Greg snorted. "I'm surprised she got one, the way she behaves."

Oh God, they're going to bring up what I did. "What d'you mean?"

Greg turned to look at her briefly, then faced the front. "She's a liar. Told porkies about some bloke touching her up. I mean, who the fuck bullshits like that, just to get someone in trouble? George threatened to slice her face if she did it again."

"Bloody hell. I wasn't aware she was that kind of girl. I only know her from nights out in the Noodle."

"She went AWOL after we paid her a visit. Nessa didn't see her in the pub for a fair old while until recently."

Hmm, I was at Haven, right under your fucking nose. "I'm moving out of her place later today anyway. I'm going back to Essex."

"Are you mental?" George asked. "You said Parker's gone there."

"Yeah, but he's in the nick. On remand for something or other, Mum said." She hoped they didn't check in with the real Vicky's parents. Shit, they wouldn't go that far, would they?

George pulled up outside Curls and Tongs, right in the planned line of fire. He'd parked opposite the door, so when Precious came along on the bike, she wouldn't be able to pause directly in front and fire through the window, if that's what the deal even was. Kayla panicked and took her phone out.

KAYLA: TAXI IN THE WAY OUTSIDE CURLS. ALICE MIGHT ALREADY BE HERE.

EVERETT: GOT IT.

"Keeping lover boy happy, are you?" George smiled at her in the rearview.

Fucking hell, he'd seen her on the phone. "Hmm."

"Go inside and wait for us. We're going to get Alice. Tell Stacey to make you a cuppa."

Kayla got out, her body a bit wobbly. This was happening. She was going to see someone gunned down, blood spraying and everything. Adrenaline brought on nausea, and she swallowed. Remembering Vicky had a bad leg from an injury caused by Parker, she limped to the salon, pausing to send another message.

KAYLA: THEY'RE GOING TO PICK HER UP NOW.

She pushed the door open. Two women in their twenties sat having their hair done, one with large curlers in, another with foils, their hairdressers young and pretty.

"Morning. You're early," Stacey said from her seat on a sofa in the waiting area. "Where's Alice?"

"George and Greg have gone to get her."

"Probably best, considering." Stacey glanced at the customers and the hairdressers as if to remind Kayla they couldn't talk about Haven here.

"Yep."

"Have a sit down. Tea? Coffee?"

"Coffee, please."

Stacey went out the back. Kayla perched on the sofa and stared outside.

A couple of kids, probably skiving school, fucked about near the litter bin. Bloody hell, should she warn Everett they were there? She didn't care if either of them got caught in the crossfire, but they'd be witnesses to Precious coming by. Would she drive past and wait farther down the road until they'd gone? Was Alice getting shot while she sat in a chair or when she left the salon? That was the bit Kayla was worried about. She'd have to make up some excuse not to leave at the same time as her, otherwise she might get shot by accident. And what if the twins stayed here, left with Alice, and one of them copped it? Kayla wasn't bothered if they died, but Everett might take it out on her if the plan went wrong, and she didn't need that kind of negativity in her life.

"You okay?" the foil customer asked.

"Yeah."

"You look a bit peaky."

Kayla smiled. "Late night."

"We were just discussing holidays before you came in. Going anywhere nice this year?"

"No."

"We're off to Tenerife." She flapped a hand towards Curler Woman. "It's going to be a right laugh."

Thankfully, Stacey came back with a coffee and placed it on the little table in front of the sofa. "Here you go. Me and my fella are going to Barbados, a Caribbean cruise. I never thought I'd get caught dead on a ship, but here we are. He assured me it's safe."

"All that water, though," Foil said. "And sharks."

"Don't," Stacey said. "I'm shit-scared of the sea."

"Do they even have sharks in the Caribbean?" Curler asked.

Of course they do, you thick bitch.

"No idea." Stacey sat beside Kayla. "Everything okay, Vicky? With…you know. I heard he turned up at you know where."

"Yeah, it was well scary that he found me, but he's in Essex now. In the nick, thank God."

"That must be a relief."

"Just a bit."

The customers talked about sunscreen, whether they should get the spray version or cream. Curler reckoned the ones with built-in tan were the best. Kayla had never liked the inane chatter when she got her hair done. She was too busy being mortified about how ugly she looked with a cape on, and she swore the mirrors were designed to make it seem like she had three chins.

She picked up her coffee and checked outside. The lads were still there. One had a lighter poised over the rubbish sticking out of the bin.

"Those fucking kids!" Stacey got up and left the salon, waving her arms about and shouting at the boys.

One stuck his middle finger up, gobbing off, then they loped away.

She came back in. "I swear to God, I'm going to ring the police on them one of these days."

Not today, not today... "They've probably gone off to set fire to something else. Little scrotes."

"They'd be stupid to. There's CCTV along here."

Kayla's heart lurched. *Does Everett know that? Or doesn't he care?*

She reminded herself she was in disguise; she'd be dumping the red wig and glasses on the way home, but what if the twins told the police Vicky had gone back to Essex? They'd look up the real person and find out someone had been impersonating her. George and Greg might go round Kayla's and ask questions about Vicky. They might not believe her answers because she'd lied to them before. The last thing she needed was them on her back.

She'd finished her coffee by the time the taxi pulled up again. Alice got out, all trainwreck in appearance. What a scruffy cow. No wonder Everett had lumped her one if she couldn't even take care of herself. Why should he have been nice to her if she couldn't even be bothered to tart herself up for him?

She entered the salon, clearly nervous, and the taxi drove away. Kayla got up and hugged Alice who hadn't even washed her hair, her greasy roots foul.

"I'm so glad you came," Kayla said.

"Me, too, although I'm shitting bricks."

"It'll be fine." Stacey rose and walked over to the chair in front of the sink. "Come and sit down. Would you like a drink?"

"No thanks." Alice sat, dropping her handbag on the floor beside the seat.

"What are we having today?" Stacey ran her fingers through the lengths of Alice's hair then gently encouraged her to rest her head back.

Alice looked at Kayla. "What do you think?"

"It needs a good trim and maybe some colour?"

Alice shrugged.

Sodding hell, she's really not bothered what she looks like. She's more depressed than when I was at Haven.

Kayla sat on the sofa again. "Do you want your nails done an' all?"

"I don't know."

Oh, for fuck's sake.

Kayla didn't have time for people like her. She wanted to shout at Alice, tell her to get a bloody grip. Move on. Stop being so insipid and sad. Still, she'd be dead soon, all her worries over. Maybe, when she saw the gun, she'd realise she had bigger things to worry about other than her hurt little feelings because her ex had bashed her about.

Stacey got on with washing Alice's hair. Kayla checked outside yet again, conscious if she kept doing it, someone might clock it. She had to act shocked when the shot was fired, so she grabbed a magazine off the table and flicked through it. Foil and Curler jabbered on about bikinis.

"I just don't like having white stripes where the straps go," Foil said.

"Then undo them while you're sunbathing."

"That's a good idea."

How thick must she be if she didn't think of that herself?

Kayla read an article about marine collagen and its benefits, glancing up when Stacey guided Alice to the cutting chair as though she were an invalid.

"Are you all right?" Kayla asked her.

"Just tired," Alice said. "I didn't sleep much last night. Worrying about coming here."

"Where have the twins gone?"

"They've got a job to do. They'll be back in a bit."

That must be why they'd had beards and wigs on. "I wonder what they're up to."

"I don't know."

You don't know anything much.

Stacey towel dried Alice's hair then combed it through. "Same style?"

"I don't mind."

Kayla took her phone out to stop herself from barking at Alice to make a fucking decision and stop being so submissive.

KAYLA: ALICE IS HERE. TWINS HAVE GONE TO DO A JOB. THEY'LL BE BACK AFTER.

EVERETT: [THUMBS-UP EMOJI]

She deleted the message string so the police wouldn't find anything if they asked to have a quick look at her phone. Everett had assured her she'd just be a witness, a friend of the deceased, so she didn't have to worry about forensics needing her mobile. Still, better to be safe than sorry.

She switched her mind to Precious who must be watching the salon, waiting for her chance to strike. Why had she come out so early when it would take a while to do Alice's hair and nails? Not knowing all the ins and outs annoyed Kayla. She wanted to be in on the finer details, to be trusted enough with them. Her stint at Haven had given her a taste for doing darker things instead of just thinking about them. Maybe, instead of running a brothel, she could be like Precious and kill for Everett, then she wouldn't have to amuse herself by daydreaming about it, she'd have firsthand experience.

The rev of a motorbike had her staring outside. Precious arrived at the kerb, leaving the engine running and putting the kickstand down. She stalked towards the salon, one arm going behind her back. Did she have the gun in a holster there? Stacey moved away from Alice, a smile in place to greet Precious, but it soon fell when Precious pushed the door wide, propping it open with her hip and aiming a gun.

The pop was loud. Alice's body shot forward, and she fell to the floor, her wheeled chair rolling to the middle of the salon. Precious left, her body language showing she was unfazed. Kayla stared at the mirror in front of where Alice had sat, blood spatter all over it.

It had all happened so quickly yet felt like slow motion.

Kayla screamed at the same time as everyone else and glanced outside. Oh shit, the lads were back, standing by the motorbike. Precious must have said something to them on her approach, her gun arm waving, and one of them held his phone up. Videoing her? She shot him in the forehead. He powered backwards from the force, crashing to the pavement, his phone skittering away, some tea leaf picking it up and slipping it in his pocket, probably to sell later. The other kid ran. Precious got on her bike and sped away, the sound of the engine muted beneath the new round of screams of the women in the salon.

"Oh my God! Oh my God!" Stacey grabbed her phone out of her pocket and dialled.

Foil and Curler ran out the back with the two hairdressers, slamming the door. Kayla supposed she ought to go and see if Alice was dead, make it look like she cared. Conscious of a crowd gathering at the window, Stacey babbling into her phone, Kayla moved a couple of steps closer, enthralled by the bloodied mirror. She could cover up her curiosity by pretending to see if Alice needed CPR. She knelt and reached out, turning Alice's head, staring at the ruined forehead where the bullet had exited. She wanted to see exposed brain, but peering too closely at it for too long would likely have Stacey wondering what the fuck was wrong with her.

For effect, Kayla let the head go and scooted back, standing to reverse to the window and lower to the sill seating. She fake sobbed, shaking, then shot up as if she couldn't bear to be near a dead body. She rushed outside so she could study the kid who must have a similar mess on his head. She couldn't see it as he lay on his back, blood pooling beneath his skull.

Onlookers had come out of the other shops, a man on his knees pinching the lad's nose and breathing air into his mouth. People cried, and someone threw up outside the little Tesco. Kayla hugged herself, darting her gaze around as if in panic, scared the biker would come back, then she ran into the salon.

"The police…they'll be here soon," Stacey said, trembling so hard her teeth chattered. "I've told the twins to stay away."

"Oh God, I can't believe my friend's dead!" Kayla sank back onto the sill seat and rocked backwards and forwards.

"This is a nightmare." Stacey plonked herself down on the sofa. "I can't…I can't look at her."

Kayla cried noisily, her gaze fixed on the blood on the mirror. Was that bits of brain on there, too? "I'm never going to see…see her a-again…"

Stacey stood and let out a long, shuddering sigh. If Kayla were in her shoes, she'd be worrying about this affecting business, annoyed that someone had been killed in her salon, giving it a bad name. She cried some more until the sound of sirens competed with the racket she made.

Stacey went to the window. "They're here."

Really? I'd never have worked that out.

Kayla held back a smile. God, she was such a nasty piece of work, and she loved it.

Chapter Ten

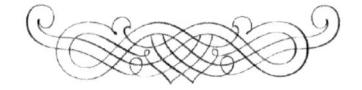

Granny and Grampy stood on the doorstep, and Everett didn't know what to do. Mum had been dead for a week. Last weekend, he'd spent it crying in his bedroom with the curtains shut, only coming out when it was time to eat. Dad had called him a cockroach, scuttling out into the light in search of food,

otherwise remaining in darkness. He kept calling him Roach now, laughing, taking the mickey.

Dad had phoned the school to say Everett was poorly and wouldn't be in all week and, while he was at work, as if nothing had happened, Everett had sat in the garden in front of the outhouse and whispered to Mum. He'd talked about all sorts, getting angry about her planning to leave him behind, something Dad had kept saying throughout the week. It was hard accepting that, when she'd been so open with him, telling him all about the new life they were going to have, even going so far as to describe the little house.

He found it difficult to like her anymore, his hatred for her growing every time Dad told him another upsetting story. Like their row when he'd come home from work early with a dicky tummy, catching her putting on her coat and shoes. If it wasn't for the suitcase and the teddy, he'd never have known she was leaving. She could have got away with it, Dad none the wiser. When he'd confronted her, she'd said she'd had enough, she wasn't putting up with him anymore, she had another fella, then she'd hit him with the bat.

Feral, Dad had called her. An adulterous slut.

Everett blinked up at his grandparents, his tummy swooping, something it did a lot now. Dad was at the supermarket, grumbling beforehand that he had to do women's work, but what choice did he have? If his wife hadn't got it into her head to fuck off, she'd still be alive, so it was her fault he had to do the shopping. Her fault he didn't know how to use the washing machine and he'd fucked it up, putting a black T-shirt in with the whites. Everything had turned grey. If he hadn't already killed her, he'd do it again for that.

Everett wasn't sure what to say. If he didn't let Granny and Grampy in, it would look weird.

"Hello, my darling. Where's Mummy?" Granny asked, a small brown suitcase at her feet.

"She left us for another man," Everett said. "She didn't come to pick me up from school, Dad had to do it."

Granny looked at Grampy. He raised his eyebrows, and she shook her head.

"You've been crying, love…" She stooped down and held her arms out.

Everett walked into them, pretending her hug was Mum's. His eyes stung, and he let out a bark of a sob. She stroked his hair; she even smelled like Mum.

Grampy cleared his throat. "Let's get inside. We'd like to speak to your father."

"Don't go in all guns blazing," Granny said, standing and guiding Everett inside. "He's the type to kick off."

Grampy picked up the case and brought it indoors. Dad wouldn't want them staying here. He'd moaned about it last time, saying after they'd left that Granny was a nosy cow and Grampy was just as bad, except he wasn't blatant about it, whatever that meant. But how could Dad tell them no without them asking questions?

"I just want to know where our daughter is." Grampy parked the case at the bottom of the stairs in the exact spot Mum had placed hers.

Tears burned the backs of Everett's eyes. He let Granny take him into the kitchen and steer him to sit at the table, the press of her hands on his shoulders something Mum used to do. She went to the kettle, so he stared out at the side of the outhouse; it didn't look any different, and if neither of them went into the garden, they wouldn't see the new bricks. It had been raining all morning, so he doubted anyone would go outside anyway. Maybe he should tell Grampy to go and look. He'd realise what had happened, then. He'd knock a hole in the bricks and see Mum on the other side.

"If you tell anyone, I'll kill you, got it?" That's what Dad kept repeating all week, holding a knife up and waggling it in Everett's face. He'd looked so angry, there was no question he meant it.

"Where's your dad?" Grampy sat at the table.

"Gone to Tesco."

"And he's left you here on your own?"

Everett shrugged. "I'm all right. I'm a big boy now."

"Eight isn't big enough to be by yourself."

Granny tutted. "Vi's just next door. She'll be keeping an ear out, I'm sure. Speaking of which... Make the tea, Gerry. I'll nip and see her now."

Everett's stomach had hurt so much since last Friday, and it hurt again now. Every time he thought about Mum, it clenched, pains spreading. "Can I come?"

"No, you stay with Grampy. I won't be long. I want to have a word before your father gets back."

<hr />

Margo strutted up Vi's path, on a mission. If Helen had told anyone else about her escape, it would be Vi, although she'd said she hadn't told anyone other than Margo and Gerry. But maybe Vi had seen or heard something. And what was this about another bloke? Was it true? Helen had been so secretive for years, so maybe that was another snippet she'd failed to mention.

When she hadn't got off the train with Everett last Friday evening, Margo had imagined something awful had happened. Shaun had likely caught her leaving and stopped her. When no one had answered the phone each time Margo had rung, alarm bells had gone off. Gerry had suggested they travel down today to get to the bottom of it. They'd come in the car, and when they found Helen, they'd be taking her and Everett back with them.

She tapped on the blue front door, oddly nervous. If Shaun came back and saw her here, he'd possibly create merry hell. At first, Margo hadn't been able to believe her ears when Helen had confessed about the beatings and abuse, but her daughter wouldn't lie about something like that, so Margo had to accept that Shaun was a bloody good actor. He'd always been pleasant in their company, so to hear he'd raised his hand to Helen plenty of times had been quite the shock.

A nasty thought entered her head. What if Helen had lied about her husband? What if she did *have another man? What if she wasn't who Margo had thought? People changed as they grew up, and it wasn't as if she could keep an eye on her daughter all the time, seeing as they'd lived up north for years.*

The door opened, and Vi stood there, her expression of worry turning into one tinged with relief. "Oh, have you heard from her?"

"No. Can I come in? I need to be quick before Shaun gets home."

Vi stepped back and walked down the hallway, leaving Margo to close the door. She went past the living room and nodded to Vi's husband lying on the sofa, a remote control in his hand. She entered the kitchen, shutting the door at Vi's gesture.

"What's going on?" *Vi asked.* "This is the first I've heard about Helen wanting to leave Shaun. He said she went the Friday before last with some fella and he hasn't heard from her since. I haven't either. I'd have thought she'd have confided in me and I'm pretty upset she didn't."

Margo lowered to a chair at the small pine table. "She said she'd kept it to herself because she couldn't risk him finding out. It took her months to get up the courage to actually do it, to even tell me. Don't take offence. She's had it tough."

"But they seemed so happy. I don't understand."

"Tell me about it. When she said he lumped her one, I couldn't believe it. I'm going to talk to Everett. Something's not right."

"He's been off school." Vi pursed her lips. *"His teacher's my friend. Mrs Watson."*

"Oh right. What was the reason?"

"He's poorly. No mention of his mother walking out."

"Maybe he was too upset, poor boy. He dotes on Helen."

"Look, no disrespect, but if Shaun's been hitting her, why didn't she tell me? We've been friends ever since they moved in yonks ago. I could have helped her."

"Some women prefer to keep it to themselves. It took her years to tell me. I had no bloody clue. There've been plenty of times she could have come clean when she was up at ours for the summer, but she never did. It wasn't until recently that she told me on the phone. We worked out an escape plan, but she left Everett behind. As for not getting off the train..." Margo caught Vi's frown; she'd forgotten the woman was in the dark. *"Helen was meant to have picked Everett up from school, taking a taxi to the train station, then getting the train to ours."*

"I see. Did Everett know?"

"I told her not to tell him, but maybe she got excited and did it anyway. He could have let it slip to Shaun."

"What are you suggesting, that Shaun stopped her?"

"That or he caught her just as she was on her way to the school. She might have been acting suspicious, and he cottoned on that something was up. Maybe she decided to leave by herself and go back for Everett another time. But there's talk she had another fella."

"What? I doubt that very much." Vi sighed. "Sorry I'm not much help. I was clueless. It wasn't until Shaun came round, asking if I knew anything about her leaving, that I was aware something was wrong. I didn't get home from work until half six so didn't see or hear anything."

Margo stood. "I'd better go. Do you have a pen and paper? I'll leave you my phone number in case you hear anything."

"Right, yes, two ticks…"

Everett hadn't answered Grampy's questions, not wanting to get anything wrong. If he was silent, then he couldn't mess up. Grampy had sat drinking tea, staring outside, then shot up when the doorbell rang. He went to answer it. Whispering filtered along the hallway, and Granny came into the kitchen.

"Did Mummy tell you she was going to move up with us?" she asked.

Everett shook his head.

"She was bringing you with her, so it's a bit of a surprise she didn't do that." She stiffened, glancing at the door.

"What's going on?" Dad said.

God, he must have put his key in the lock really quietly.

"We've come to help you with Everett for the weekend." Grampy. "It's got to be tough, looking after him on your own. I've just made a cuppa."

He sounded nice, as if he wasn't just moaning about Dad and calling him names when Granny had been next door. What was it? A cunting fucking bastard?

They entered the kitchen, Grampy with a load of Tesco bags, Dad lifting a hand to scratch his head, giving Everett one of his mean looks behind it so no one else saw, then shifting his sights to Granny and smiling at her.

"All right, Margo? Have you heard from her?" Dad went to sit next to her. "I've been going out of my mind with worry."

"So have we," Granny said, "seeing as no one's been answering the phone."

"I couldn't face it." Dad rubbed a hand down his face. *"I've been that gutted, plus Everett's been poorly."*

"So I heard."

Dad frowned. *"Oh right?"*

Granny didn't explain how she knew that. *"Have you heard from her?"*

"Not since I saw her on the Friday, no."

"What, exactly, did she say to you?"

"That she'd had enough, she was leaving. Got herself another man."

"Why had she had enough, though?"

Dad shrugged. *"Search me. That's what I've been trying to work out. I thought we were happy."*

"She told me you hit her on the regular."

Dad's mouth dropped open. *"You what? Are you having a bloody laugh?"*

"No. I don't find any of this remotely funny. Helen tells me you're abusive, that she's going to leave you, and when she doesn't get off the train with Everett, what am I supposed to believe?"

"I have no idea."

"Did you phone the police?"

"Why, when she said she was leaving me? They can't stop her or force her to come back. She went of her own free will."

"If I don't hear from her for another week, then I'm phoning it in," Grampy said. "Do you want me to put this shopping away? Some's frozen, and it might melt if we leave it out much longer."

Dad got up and helped him, answering their questions and sounding like he was upset about Mum. Everett watched and listened, wanting to say something but not daring to. He glanced outside, Mum so close, yet Granny and Grampy didn't know.

Everett wished he *didn't.*

Chapter Eleven

Precious had dropped the bike, gear, and gun at the specified place. She'd watched it being loaded into the back of a black Transit, then the driver had dropped her off on a residential street with no CCTV. She currently walked around town in her shorts, T-shirt, and flip-flops, a bumbag hanging at her waist. At the time, she hadn't cared one jot about shooting that stupid kid who'd held his phone up in front of her—he'd annoyed her, and her instinct had been to eliminate him—but now she'd calmed down, she reckoned it could pose a problem. Roach wasn't going to be happy when he found out what she'd done, but he knew what she was like. Her knee-jerk reactions were a bone of contention between them. As for the twins... Fuck, they were going to be raging if they ever caught up with her. A child being killed meant they'd ramp up their efforts to find her.

After buying a few clothes from New Look and a dress from Roman, she entered the Red Lion and ordered a Coke and a sandwich. She thanked the landlord, popped her bags on the floor, and sat at the bar so she could see the door. It had been two hours since she'd fired the shots, and her feet ached from tromping into the shops to get herself seen. Her sandwich arrived, doorstep bread slices, and she munched while she thought about her life so far. If it wasn't for Roach, she wouldn't have gone down this road. As kids, they'd hung around together with Boycie, but at secondary school, she'd broken away from them and made friends of her own. Turned out they were two-faced bitches, but whatever, she had nothing to do with them now.

At eighteen, Roach had seen her in a club and asked if she wanted to be a part of a business he was setting up. That it involved drugs didn't bother her. If people were stupid enough to waste their money buying them, that was their problem. She'd been a runner, dossing in the flat Roach now rented out to her. The only catch to her living there permanently was she had to let Roach and Boycie meet to discuss shit, and as she'd now moved on from drugs to the brothel, she wasn't indoors much to hear about what they were up to anyway.

She had, however, been there when Alice's murder had been brought up. Of course, she'd offered her services, eager for a thrill. She'd killed for Roach before, scumbags who owed him drug money, a quick slice to their throat ending their pathetic lives, and shooting Alice hadn't fazed her in the way it should—you know, guilt at actually taking someone's life. She *had* felt sorry for her, though.

She'd never met the woman but believed what Roach had said about her. After all, he'd never lied to her before, and Boycie had backed him up, saying Alice was a bit dim whenever he went round there and she'd fucked up a lot. Mainly her bad cooking or buying the wrong wine. Still, like Boycie, Precious agreed that Alice hadn't done anything to deserve being killed. But she valued her income too much to press the point more than she already had, and with Alice dead, Roach would look for a new woman, leaving Precious alone.

She cared for him but didn't much like him anymore. Shagging him no longer appealed, but she did it just the same. Probably because of some misguided need to be wanted, desired. Stupid, when he always dumped her as soon as he got tired of her. She made out it didn't upset her, but it kind of did. More and more lately, she was seeing Roach for exactly who he was—someone who was only out for himself. He didn't care who he hurt along the way.

She wanted a proper man, a proper relationship. She prayed he'd find a woman who did as she was told for long enough to give Precious time to do that. Problem was, what kind of bloke would set up home with a bird like her? And Roach would likely vet him, shit the life out of him when he threatened to stab him silly if he ever blabbed about what went on. Because having a man in her life would mean he'd know the ins and outs, or at least some of them. She wouldn't lie about who she was—well, maybe she wouldn't admit to being a murderer, but whoever she shacked up with would know she worked at the brothel.

Sandwich finished, she sipped her Coke. She'd been cocking an ear for any word about the shooting, but none of the customers near her had said anything about it. The salon wasn't that far away, so surely news should have spread by now.

That old tart came in, the one who sang here at weekends sometimes. Laundrette Lil. Today, her outfit was enough to damage Precious' retinas it was that loud. Red-and-white-striped leggings, an orange floaty top with pink spots, and high-heeled sandals in an alarming shade of neon green. None of it matched, and all of it clashed with an obvious purple wig.

Lil rushed up to the bar and leaned her forearms on it, breathless. "Did you hear what's gone on, Dave?"

The landlord frowned. "Nope, but I'm sure you're going to tell me."

"There's only been a fucking shooting."

Precious gasped. "Oh God, this Estate just keeps getting worse. What happened?"

Lil turned to her, clearly pleased to have an avid audience, not only in Dave and Precious but a few others at the bar, too. "Some fucker on a motorbike came along, and the rider went into Curls and Tongs and killed a woman. But that's not the best of it. They also shot a lad outside. What's this place coming to, eh? The biker drove off, and you can bet they won't be caught. Fake plates, someone said."

"How would they even know that?" Dave asked.

Lil shrugged. "Don't ask me, I'm just reporting what I heard. Maybe the number and letter sequence was wrong or something. It was a skinny bloke apparently, the shooter. Not very tall."

"Didn't he have a helmet on, then?" Precious asked. "I mean, how could they tell it was a man?"

"Face covered or not, you can tell a bloke from a woman, can't you. And honestly, can you see a woman doing that? Being a fucking hitman? Or hitwoman, rather?"

"Hit *person* these days," Dave said.

Lil frowned. "What are you on about?"

"Doesn't matter." Dave leaned on the bar. "So what's the score now?"

"Stands to reason the twins are going to be gunning for them. They'll be after whoever did this, especially because the woman who was shot is a friend of theirs."

Friend, my arse. "Oh no…"

Lil nodded. "Yeah, so you can imagine how they feel."

"I wouldn't want to be in their shoes." *Or is that flip-flops…* Precious bit her lip to stop herself from laughing.

"Me neither." Lil smiled at Dave. "Anyway, a double voddy and tonic, please, and whatever you're having. I've given myself some time off and got my nails done in that new bar down the road." She held her hand up to reveal yellow polish with blue gems at the tips.

Jesus, someone send her to fashion school, for fuck's sake.

"Very nice." Dave turned away to pour her vodka from an optic.

Lil sank onto a stool. "I'm that shaken up by the shooting. It had to be a hit because of the way the biker only shot one woman in the salon. If they were mad in the head like that spree-killer copper who went round recently, they'd have shot everyone, surely. Mind you, there's that lad who copped it, too."

It had dominated the news, some detective called Flint going off his rocker and popping loads of people. Apparently, he'd been involved in that teenager's suicide an' all, Summer someone. He'd groomed her on a teen website, the filthy bastard. Precious had no sympathy for anyone involved. Summer shouldn't have tried to be a woman while she was still a girl, and her parents should have monitored her internet use properly. All of it could have been prevented. It was curious, though, how the majority of the men killed in the spree had something to do with women who lived at Haven. Roach hadn't passed on any snippets about whether that was a coincidence or not, so maybe Kayla hadn't been privy to any conversations regarding that while she'd been there.

The twins ought to watch themselves. Kayla had said they'd talked freely about some things in front of the women, trusting them because they'd been warned not to open their mouths.

They believed in people too much. She reckoned they ought to sail a tighter ship. Still, if it was tighter, they'd have discovered who Kayla really was. Mind you, her disguise as Vicky was brilliant. She looked and sounded nothing like Kayla.

Precious needed to go home soon. The police would come round eventually, asking her about Roach as Everett, and she'd have to tell them they were a couple. Make out he'd never said a bad word about Alice, so why the hell would he have her killed? As for her own side of things, she didn't harbour any ill-will, so she wouldn't have killed her either.

Lil nudged her. "'Ere, cop an eyeful of those two. They've been crying."

Precious stared at who'd just walked in. What the fuck was *she* doing here? Wouldn't it look off that she'd witnessed her mate being shot and now she was down the boozer? Maybe she'd come for a drink to steady her nerves.

Kayla and Stacey walked to a table near the bar and sat.

Precious ordered another Coke, wanting to stay for a bit longer so she could see what Kayla, looking like Vicky, was up to. She might say something about the shooting—she could turn out to be a fucking liability.

Stacey took their drinks over to her and sat, putting the glasses on the table then patting Kayla's hand. Kayla wasn't in the same clothes as earlier—she'd likely had to hand her outfit over to the police—and what she had on now was clearly not her own stuff. Some kind of workout gear, pink Lycra. Her trainers looked too big. Had Stacey lent her something? Kayla rubbed her upper arms, glancing around, perhaps scoping the place out to see who was there. She didn't appear comfortable.

Kayla caught Precious' eye and gave her the kind of stare that said: *I had no choice but to come here.* Right. So Stacey had suggested they have a drink? Understandable, they'd witnessed two murders, and the salon would be closed, what with it being a crime scene.

"Are you feeling calmer now?" Stacey asked her.

Lil nudged Precious again. "Eyes peeled, ears wide open."

Kayla sighed. "It was awful. I'll have nightmares for the rest of my life."

"Me, too." Stacey sipped some of her drink. "Do you think it was a hit? They went straight for Alice like they knew she'd be there."

"I don't understand how they'd know, because the twins made sure she was safe. I don't get it. Maybe it was random."

Lil stared over. "Are you on about that shooting?"

Stacey nodded.

Lil got off her stool and gestured for Precious to do the same. From the side of her mouth she said to Precious, "We'll go and find shit out for The Brothers, come on."

In a situation she really didn't need to be in, Precious collected her bags and followed Lil to the table. They sat in the spare chairs, and Lil swigged some of her vodka.

"Tell me exactly what happened," she said. "I'm friends with the twins, and they'll need to know everything, if you catch my drift. I can pass it on for you."

"George has already rung me," Stacey said. "We're meeting them in a bit. I just needed some alcohol to help me get over the shock, and this place seemed as good as any."

"They'll catch whoever did this, hands down." Lil let out a long breath, a strand of her wig flapping. "Whoever it is will be dead inside a week, you'll see."

Precious didn't think so. Roach had been a mastermind with this, but still, a frisson of fear swept through her tummy. She wasn't stupid enough to think he'd have her back if the shit hit the fan. He'd think nothing of letting her take the fall for this if he had to, claiming innocence while she was in a cell. But despite their past and friendship, she wouldn't keep her mouth shut where he was concerned either. If it came to it, she'd grass him up in a heartbeat.

He thought he had her wrapped around his little finger, but he didn't. She was out for herself as much as he was, and he'd soon learn that if he even thought about putting her name forward to save his own skin. Boycie wouldn't blindly follow Roach either. All three of them were strong-willed and selfish. They'd claimed loyalty to one another all those years ago, but that would be swept to the wayside if push came to shove. She didn't think Roach realised that, though. He acted as if she and Boycie were his lackeys, something she'd never liked. He'd do well to realise they were all on a level footing. Just because he paid their wages, it didn't mean he was the boss of their fucking lives.

Maybe she ought to speak to Boycie privately, feel him out, see if he had the same thoughts she did.

"What if more people other than the shooter were involved?" Stacey said. "I get it that some people work by themselves, especially if they're a hitman or whatever, but if Alice was the target and not a random victim, then other people must have known she'd be at the salon."

Kayla stiffened. "I knew. It was me who asked her to go there. I just wanted to do something special for her, make her feel better about herself. God, do you think the police reckon I'm in on it?"

"Of course not." Stacey laid a hand on Kayla's. "You were *friends*."

"Who's Alice, the bird who copped it?" Lil asked.

"Yeah." Kayla sipped her drink.

Precious could have clapped; the conversation was going so well and to her advantage. "My boyfriend's ex-wife is an Alice." She bit her lip. "God, I hope it isn't her. He'll be gutted. They might be divorced, but he still cares about her."

"Bloody awful business." Lil looked at Kayla. "So you met her at the salon today, did you?"

Kayla nodded. "The twins dropped me off then went to pick her up. I was at a refuge with her for a while. I got my life sorted, but she wasn't ready to leave yet. I've let the police know I'm moving back to Essex later today, so they'll just have to contact me there if they need to speak to me again."

"I thought I detected an accent." Lil stared at her, head cocked. "Sounds to me, if you were in a refuge, that whoever Alice was running from must have killed her. The simple solution is usually the truth. Occam's razor."

Kayla glanced at Precious, clearly appealing for help.

Precious made a quick decision. This could help them both out. "Who was she running from? What's his name?"

"Her husband," Kayla said. "Everett. I told the police about him."

As per the plan, so nothing to be alarmed about there.

"Everett? I'm seeing someone called that." Precious frowned, feigning worry.

"Fuck me, it could be the same fella," Lil said. "There aren't that many Everetts about with an ex called Alice, are there. You'd better watch yourself. If it's him, dragging you into this mess... Trust me, men are a fucking nightmare. We're better off without them."

Stacey piped up and said to Vicky, "Did you tell Kayla you were meeting Alice today?"

"*That* bitch?" Lil barked. "If it's the same bitch I'm thinking of."

"Barnes," Kayla said.

Lil nodded. "That's the one. How do you know *her*?"

"I've been kipping on her sofa at her flat," Kayla said, "and she isn't a bitch. And no, I didn't tell her where I was going or who with because, well, it'd be dumb when Alice was hiding at the refuge. Everything has to be kept hush-hush so the women are safe. I'm not a div."

"That Kayla's a cow," Lil said, "and no one can change my mind on that. I heard she got men to touch her up then cried wolf."

Kayla stiffened again. "I don't know her that well. I met her in a pub, and she offered for me to sleep at hers until I got myself sorted. She's been nice to me. She's hardly the type to arrange a murder when she doesn't even know Alice."

"How do you know?" Lil seemed suspicious. "What if *she's* seeing this Everett, too? No offence," she said to Precious, "but men are dogs. They'll poke anyone with a pulse."

"I'd better get hold of him." Precious stood, picked up her bags, and left the pub. The sun greeted her with its savage heat, and she took her phone out. She messaged Everett on her personal contract phone so it would look legitimate if the police asked to check her mobile.

PRECIOUS: I DON'T WANT TO ALARM YOU, BUT I WAS JUST IN THE RED LION, AND TWO WOMEN CAME IN SAYING SOMEONE CALLED ALICE WAS SHOT AT THE HAIRDRESSER'S THIS MORNING. ONE OF THEM MENTIONED ALICE'S EX IS CALLED EVERETT. WHAT IF IT'S HER? HAVE THE POLICE CONTACTED YOU? IF NOT, MAYBE GET HOLD OF THEM. I'M SO SHOCKED, POOR THING.

He didn't respond, so maybe he was with the police now.

She shrugged, popped her phone away, and walked along the street, nipping into Superdrug to buy some shampoo. He'd understand why she'd contacted him, that she'd had no choice. For all they knew, Lil or Stacey could pass on the information to the police or the twins that Precious was seeing a man named Everett. If she hadn't texted him after hearing the news, it would look weird.

She left the shop, waiting for a bus home.

There was nothing she could do now but wait.

Chapter Twelve

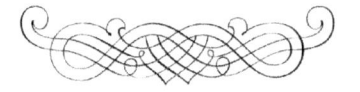

Kayla had just wanted to go home after the police had finished speaking to her outside the salon, but Stacey had suggested they go for a drink. That Lil woman kept looking at her funny an' all. Was she suspicious? Had Kayla been acting oddly? She didn't think so. And as for Lil saying Kayla was a bitch and a cow…

You have no idea what a cow I can be, lady.

Precious getting her to mention Everett's name must have been for a reason. Kayla could ask him or her later, she supposed, but so long as her part in this was over, did she really care? The police would soon realise she'd given them someone else's name, and maybe they'd come to see Kayla to ask about the so-called Vicky, seeing as she'd let them know where she'd been staying. Maybe that had been a stupid move, but there was nothing she could do about that now. And anyway, she could handle the police as Kayla. There was nothing to worry about.

She'd go home, shower, and wash the yoga clothes Stacey had given her. She'd pop them back to the salon at some point, whenever it reopened. The problem was, if only Alice had been murdered, it would likely have been a clear-cut case, but that boy... Kayla would never forget the state of him on that pavement.

But he should have minded his own business. He got himself killed. Stupid little twat.

"Will you be okay, going to Essex on the train and whatever later?" Stacey asked.

It felt odd to have someone genuinely concerned about her. Cooper was nicer than any man she'd been with before, but he wasn't exactly Prince Charming all the time.

Kayla smiled. "Yeah, I'll let Mum know what's happened. She'll take the afternoon off, I expect, be there for when I get home."

Lil stared at Kayla again. "How come you're in London, sofa-surfing at Kayla's? How come you were at refuge here and not Essex?"

None of your fucking business. "I moved here with my ex for work. He's in the nick now, so I can go back."

"Right…" Lil didn't appear to believe her.

Stop being paranoid. "I'll be glad to get out of here. London's been nothing but trouble."

"Why, because of the shooting?" Lil sniffed. "I should imagine it was quite the shock. You know, her being your mate, you being one of the only ones to know she'd be there."

Kayla's heart rate sped up. "What are you saying? Are you accusing me of setting this up?"

"If the cap fits. Just so you know, I'll be passing the contents of this conversation to The Brothers."

"Do what you like. It was nothing to do with me. There's loads of people at the refuge, it could have been one of them. The police will look into it."

"So will George and Greg." Lil got up. "See you around."

She left the pub, taking her gaudy outfit and hideous hair with her.

"Blimey," Stacey muttered. "She's a bit intense. If she knew you, there's no way she'd think you had anything to do with it."

"Maybe she's generally a suspicious old cow." Kayla laughed. "No disrespect, but she's a bit much, isn't she."

Kayla had seen Lil around, knew her name from those stupid posters of hers plastered to the windows, advertising the fact she'd be singing here. Seemed Lil knew about Kayla, too. It was a small world.

"She likely means well," Stacey said. "She's good friends with the twins, so it's obvious she'd be asking questions on their behalf. Still..." She checked her watch. "We'd better get to the Noodle. We should have gone there in the first place instead of coming here."

They walked there, barely talking. Kayla supposed Stacey was coming to terms with the loss of business, which would be at the forefront of Kayla's mind if she were in her shoes. Was Stacey secretly raging that her salon was closed?

Or was she the genuine type who'd be more saddened that two people had lost their lives?

They entered the car park at the back of the Noodle, and Kayla's stomach went over at the sight of the twins' taxi. She just had one more part to play as Vicky, then that persona could disappear. In the back of the taxi, she felt sick as George and Greg partially turned in their seats to look at her.

"What the *fuck* happened?" George asked. "You asked Alice to go and get her hair and nails done, then she gets shot? Make this make sense, because at the moment, you're top of our suspect list."

Kayla switched on the waterworks. "Me? I didn't do anything! She was one of the best mates I ever had. If you think I could so something like that…"

"Calm down, bruv," Greg said.

"Where's Parker?" George asked her. "Is he *really* in the nick? Was that hit meant for you and they got the wrong person?"

"I told you, Mum said he got arrested. It couldn't have been him. And anyway, what about that kid who got shot, too?"

"He was collateral damage by all accounts," Greg said. "Silly boy was filming the shooter leaving the salon. The fact the hitman had a helmet on and couldn't be recognised, you'd think they'd have realised the kid wasn't a threat, but maybe it was a knee-jerk reaction. They panicked, forgetting they even had the helmet on, which would suggest they're a novice."

Kayla wiped tears off her cheeks with the back of her hand. "Well, it wasn't anything to do with me. I *loved* Alice. She was my best friend at Haven."

"God knows why," George said, "because you were one angry bitch when you stayed there."

"Wouldn't you be if you'd been beaten up by your other half?" Stacey butted in. "God, she was hardly likely to be all sunshine and roses, was she."

"I agree," Greg said, staring at George. "Button it if you can't keep your thoughts to yourself. I'll start calling you Edna if you're not careful."

George sighed. "I'm just angry. For Alice. That kid. We've got to go and see his parents, offer them help with the funeral." He made eye contact with Kayla. "I apologise for being arsey."

She nodded her acceptance but wished she could tell him to go and fuck himself.

Stacey ran a hand through her hair. "There's something you should know. Laundrette Lil was in the Red Lion, so she'll probably get hold of you, but she was with this woman who said she's seeing a man called Everett who has an ex-wife called Alice."

George pinched the bridge of his nose. "Yeah, we're aware of who he is. He's next on our list to beat up, but we can't exactly do it at the minute. We're going to see him soon; we're waiting for the police to speak to him first. Our source has told us they're going to see him at his office. Who's the woman?"

"No idea," Stacey said.

"We'll ask Lil. Odd that she hasn't texted us about it yet." George didn't look too happy about that. "We're aware of Everett having a bird, so it's likely her, but who knows, he might have another on the go. Right, we want to know what went down from start to finish."

Stacey took over, relating the events, and Kayla remained quiet, acting sad. When it was her turn, she cried between sentences, especially when she came to the part about checking whether Alice was alive.

"It was horrible." She sniffled. "So much blood…"

They chatted for a while longer, then George told them they'd be in touch.

Not with Vicky, you won't.

Chapter Thirteen

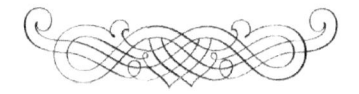

Lil had to get her head straight before she contacted the twins. She'd rushed to her laundrette and currently sat in the little room out the back, nursing a cup of tea. She'd gone there instead of home because she didn't like people in her gaff, and the twins would likely want to speak to her face to face about this. Her staff hadn't questioned why she'd come into work during her time off, but she'd said she wanted to check the books as a way to get them to leave her in peace.

Just do it. Get hold of them. If you're wrong, no harm done, but if you're right…

LIL: GOT SOME NEWS FOR YOU REGARDING THE SALON SHOOTING—I ASSUME YOU'VE HEARD ABOUT IT? SOME WOMAN WHO WAS AT YOUR REFUGE, I SAW HER IN THE RED LION. SHE SEEMED SUSS. CAN'T PUT MY FINGER ON IT, BUT THERE'S SOMETHING OFF ABOUT HER. SHE'S BEEN KIPPING AT KAYLA BARNES' PLACE. CALL ME MISS MARPLE, BUT MY DETECTIVE SENSES WENT ON HIGH ALERT.

GG: WE WONDERED WHEN YOU'D GET HOLD OF US. YOU TOOK YOUR TIME.

LIL: I HAD TO HAVE A THINK, SEE IF I WAS SEEING THINGS THAT WEREN'T THERE.

GG: WHERE ARE YOU?

LIL: AT THE LAUNDRETTE. COME ROUND THE BACK.

Feeling better that she'd got that off her chest, she finished her tea and waited. It didn't take long for a tap to sound on the back door, and she got up to unlock it. After letting them in, she wandered back to the sofa, leaving them the chairs at the table.

"What's got your radar bleeping?" George asked, taking a pew.

Greg stood at the kitchenette making coffee, the kettle still hot from her using it. "You think Kayla's involved?"

"Gawd knows," Lil said, "but isn't it best you check it out anyway?"

George nodded and drew the biscuit tin towards him. He popped the lid off and took out a custard cream. "She's a fucking little cow, but murder?"

Lil agreed, but… "I know, but you can't be too sure. People hide behind façades."

George stared at her. "Like you do."

"Yep. You'd never have known I'd killed men if I hadn't told you."

"True." He bit a chunk off his biscuit and chewed.

"Personally," Greg said, "I don't think Kayla's got it in her to organise a piss-up in a brewery, let alone a hit—and word has it that was a professional job. And why would she want to kill Alice anyway?"

Lil shrugged. "I don't know, do I! Fucking hell, you asked me to pass info on, and I've done it. It's your job to sort it out."

"I'd have punched anyone else for talking to us like that," George said.

"Yeah, and I'd punch you right back, so knob off. Look, she was weird, all right? As for the bird who's seeing an Everett, she seemed nice, worried that if it *was* your Alice, he'd be upset she's been offed."

"From what Alice told us, him being upset is highly unlikely. Who's the bird, do you know?"

"I've seen her in the pub a few times, she's aways on her own, but I couldn't tell you who she is. She'd been shopping, I know that much. She had bags with her. Maybe Stacey knows her."

"We've not long seen her. She never said anything about Vicky being off."

Lil frowned. "Vicky?"

"She's Alice's friend, the one you're suss about."

"Right."

Greg came over with the coffees on a tray. He placed it on the table and handed Lil a cup. "Vicky was a gobby mare at the refuge, really angry, but that's understandable, given what she went through. She was far from angry today. Lost, I'd say, and bloody gutted about her mate dying. She didn't seem off to me at all."

"That's because you haven't got a woman's intuition," Lil said. "I'm telling you, there's something not right there."

George glanced at Greg. "Maybe we should speak to her without Stacey there. If she's staying with Kayla…"

Greg sat. "We'll nip round to hers in a few."

George picked up another biscuit. "She's shit-scared of us, so it won't take much to get info out of her, providing she even knows any."

They chatted for a bit and, coffees drunk, the biscuit tin lighter, what with Greg nicking a load of bourbons and Jammy Dodgers, the twins left. Lil exited via the front, needing to go home and ponder, although she cursed herself for letting this bug her. She didn't want to deal with crap anymore, she'd had a lifetime of it, yet here she was, diving into a ruddy great pile of it.

Fuck's sake.

Chapter Fourteen

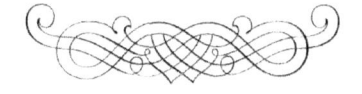

Roach sat in his fake work office, two detectives in the chairs opposite. One, DS Colin Broadley, the other, DI Nigel Hampton. Colin appeared bored, and Roach sensed he didn't like the copper he was with. He was good at reading people's body language, and Colin was irritated. Nigel, on the other hand, was a serious sort, intent on getting down to business, obvious by the way he sat ramrod straight and his general demeanour of a man on a mission.

"How can I help you?" Roach asked.

"Firstly," Nigel said in a Liverpudlian accent, "I'd like to ask about your relationship with Alice Sikes."

So she kept her married name, then. "My ex-wife? We divorced amicably, as far as anyone else is concerned. I didn't give her any hassle there."

"What do you mean by that?" Nigel asked.

"No one knew what went on behind closed doors, and I wanted to keep it that way. I never wanted her to be tarred with a certain brush."

"Can you be clearer, please?"

"She beat me up regularly." He winced as if admitting that was painful.

Nigel seemed flummoxed. "Oh. Right."

Roach continued. "Prior to the divorce, we had our ups and downs like any other couple, but because she had mental health and alcohol issues it was worse. Why?"

"Mental health issues?"

"Hmm, she accused *me* of abusing *her*. I didn't. I told her she needed help, to go and see a doctor."

"I see. When was your last interaction with her?"

"God, it's been a while. I saw her in a Tesco car park one day, got to be about six months ago?" He'd seen her in that scabby flat she'd rented, but whatever. If she'd reported him for violence, no officers had come to see him about it, so it was safe to say these men here didn't know. "I asked her how she was, and she said she'd settled somewhere. She seemed happy, even laughed a few times when she told me about her job and someone who works there; a right joker, apparently."

"So despite her saying you abused her, she was okay enough to chat to you."

"Yep. Hardly the actions of someone scared of me, is it. The thing is with Alice, she's all swings and roundabouts." He thought about Edna and how she behaved. "Personally, I think she's bipolar. One minute she's okay, the next she's not right. Not being rude, but why are you here?"

"Sadly, Alice passed away this morning."

Roach sat bolt upright. "What? Oh God, don't tell me she went through with it."

A frown scored Nigel's forehead. "Through with what?"

"She threatened to kill herself several times during our marriage. Poor woman. Is that what happened?"

"No, she was shot while getting her hair done."

"Shot? What the hell? Who'd want to do *that*?"

"That's what we aim to find out. Where were you this morning between nine and, say, eleven?"

"I was at the Noodle with my neighbour for breakfast. I arrived here at the office about half eleven."

"Is there CCTV for this place?"

"Yes. The man on the security desk downstairs will help you out. Are you saying you suspect *me*? I can assure you, even though Alice accused me of all sorts, I still cared about her. I'd never do anything to hurt her."

"We have to ask that question," Nigel said. "Elimination purposes. What's your neighbour's name and address?"

"Max Potter. Twenty-four Gladstone Close."

"Thanks. Did Alice contact you at all after the Tesco interaction?"

"No, and I haven't contacted her either. Why would I? We're divorced. I'm with someone else now, I've moved on."

"And who are you in a relationship with?"

"Precious Granger."

"And her address?"

Roach gave it. "God, you're not insinuating *she* did this, are you?"

"Err, no, but we'd like to speak to her all the same. We're ruling people out. Were you aware Alice went to stay at a refuge?"

"Eh? Why would anyone even tell me that? What was she doing there, maintaining the illusion that I've been beating her up?"

"It would appear so. We've spoken to the owner, Sharon, and she confirms Alice was afraid of you."

"I never laid a hand on her at any time."

"With no evidence, we're hard pressed to prove what she's said is true. Still, you can understand us following it up. There's motive—she's supposedly lied about you, and you've arranged for her to be shot to shut her up. *Not* that I'm saying that's what happened, but you can see how it looks."

"Of course, but it wasn't me."

"Is there anything else we might need to know about her?"

"She's—was—troubled."

"We're aware. She'd been seeing a therapist at the refuge. We'll be visiting him later."

"Good, then maybe he'll give you an insight."

Colin eyed Roach funny. "Why would she say you'd abused her if you hadn't?"

Roach sighed. "Look, I didn't want to speak ill of the dead, but it seems I'm going to have to. It became clear after we married that if she didn't get her own way, she'd do whatever she could to get it. She even accused one of our neighbours of spying on her. He lives opposite me, next door to Max, and she said he was a pervert, looking into our bedroom window while she was naked after a shower. Her imagination is unreal."

"But we only have your word for that," Colin said.

Roach sighed. "Not at all. She phoned the police on him. There'll be a record of it. And I have recordings to back up my abuse claim if that's any help. Hang on." He woke his laptop up and clicked on a file, finding the videos he'd filmed without Alice's knowledge, two of his gaslighting stints he'd engineered on purpose, something he'd watched later and smiled over. "She was getting worse with the accusations at this point, so I filmed her—call it insurance, I don't know, but I needed something to prove *I* wasn't the monster. You'll be able to see how unhinged she could be." He turned the laptop around so they could see it and pressed PLAY, leaning round to view it himself.

"If you hit me again, I'm going to the police." Alice stared at him, her eyes red from crying. She breathed heavily, an angry animal ready to claw at him.

Silly cow.

"Hit you? I've never hit you. Please, just stop it. It isn't funny, keep saying I've punched you when I haven't."

"But you did."

"When?"

"Half an hour ago!"

"What? How can I have done that when I've only just got home from work? I've literally just walked through the front door." He shook his head. "Seriously, love, you need to go and see someone. This is the fifth time you've accused me of doing this, and it isn't fair. Next you'll be telling the neighbours, but thank God they won't believe you because of what you said about him over the road."

"He was perving on me."

"He was painting his windowsill! You called the police on someone who was only doing DIY. He's a judge, for God's sake."

"So? People in jobs like that do bad things all the time."

"Can you hear yourself? You're changing things to fit your narrative. You're going to get an innocent person arrested if you keep on. Like me."

"You're not innocent, though."

"Alice, I love you, so why would I hit you? It doesn't make sense."

"You're a liar!"

She launched at him, and he let her, scraping her nails down his face then punching his nose. Cartilage crunched, and hot blood fell from his nostrils, rolling over his lips. He cuffed it with his suit jacket sleeve, staring down at the red stain.

"Alice, this can't go on. I've kept this quiet for too long now. You're the one abusing me."

She sobbed. "Oh my God, I can't cope with this." She sank to her knees and cried on the carpet.

Roach got down there with her, cradling her in his arms. "It'll be okay. You don't know what you're doing when you have these episodes, and when you come out of it, you're always sorry and confused. We'll see the doctor together, all right?"

"I need help, someone help me, please, oh God…"

"Yes, you need help, and we'll get it."

"Please…please."

"Come on, I'll make you some tea."

He helped her up and guided her out of the room. Thirty seconds passed, then he came back, ensuring his bloodied nose was in full view as he reached for his phone propped on the mantelpiece. He recited the date and time, sighing afterwards, a defeated man.

The recording blanked out.

"Right, well…" Nigel, eyebrows raised, seemed incredulous.

"Who divorced who?" Colin asked.

Roach grimaced. "She divorced me, for unreasonable behaviour, would you believe. It should have been the other way around."

"And you just accepted the blame?"

"I know how it sounds, but you weren't in my shoes. I wanted a divorce as much as her by then, so yes, if it meant we were no longer married and I didn't have to suffer, I signed whatever. I came out looking like the bad guy, but as you'll see when you dig deeper, she never told any of her family about the so-called abuse I dished out, only two of her friends who encouraged her to leave me. I don't blame them for giving her that advice, people will always believe a woman over a man in these situations. I mean, look at me. I'm a big bloke and she's a small woman. No one would believe she was the one doing the punching."

"Why did you keep it quiet?" Colin asked.

"I didn't want people to think badly of her. I loved her, despite what she did. Do you want to see the other video?"

Nigel nodded. "Please, and if we can take copies…"

"No problem." Roach hid a smile and clicked PLAY.

"You're doing it again, Alice. Jesus, I can't cope with this." He stood side-on to the phone recording them, cupping his eye. *"Please just pack it in. I don't know why you keep hitting me, and I don't know why you keep saying it's me doing it to you."*

She'd not long punched him in the face, her rage at him bigger than it had ever been, her courage in sticking up for herself proof that he'd pushed her to her limit and she no longer worried about the repercussions from him. He'd landed a thump to her gut as soon as he'd got home from work (she'd pissed him off yet again), and she'd sat at the kitchen table, drinking a bottle of wine between sobs while he'd called her all the names under the sun, nice and quietly so the neighbours didn't hear.

He lowered his hand and side-shuffled to the mirror, watching her as if he expected her to attack him if he turned his back. Like he was worried, scared of her. He did turn then, staring into the mirror above the mantel, hoping the camera got a good shot of his burgeoning black eye. He caught sight of her reflection. She ran at him, leaping onto his back, her hands around his throat.

"You fucking bastard! I hate you!"

He created overdramatic choking sounds, lifting one hand to try and get one of hers free. "You're hurting me," he croaked out. "Please, stop… Get off!"

She kept one hand at his throat, raising the other to slap at his head. He winced, walking backwards to ensure the camera caught it all. Her face…she'd become a crazed animal, her mouth twisted, eyes wide.

"I'll fucking kill you," she seethed. "It's the only way…"

"Please…oh God, please don't do this…"

He managed to loosen her grip on his neck, and she flailed, her balance shot. She fell backwards, landing on the floor. He crouched to draw her to the far end of the room so the camera would pick up what they were doing, taking her hand.

"Are you okay? Did you hurt yourself?"

"What do you care?" Her slurred words proved how much she'd drunk.

"Of course I care."

"I don't know who I am anymore," she wailed, her mouth a gaping hole, tears spilling.

"It's all right, you've just had another episode, that's all. Deep breaths."

"Why do you want to be with me when—"

"Because I love you, that's why. Up you get, onto the sofa. Sleep that drink off, okay? You're always like this when you have a whole bottle of wine."

"You've got a black eye."

"I know."

"Good." She laughed as she lay back, her hilarity spurred to hysterical levels by booze. "I'm glad I hit you. You deserve it. You're nothing but a piece of shit."

She'd pay for that later, but for now, he'd let it slide. "Why do you always call me names?"

"Because…"

"Shh, sleep."

He stroked her hair, and she drifted off quickly. He sat and fake cried for around thirty seconds, wrenching sobs, then got up and said the time and date, switching the camera off.

Nigel seemed uncomfortable. "Did she drink often?"

"Every day. Functioning alcoholic."

"And you came home to her drunk?"

"Yes."

"Were there ever any raised voices?"

"No, I'm not the type, and she wouldn't have shouted because otherwise the neighbours would have heard her. None of them ever asked any questions because as far as they were aware, we were the perfect couple. When she left me, they thought she'd gone missing and brought food round, looked after me; they must have felt sorry for me, but I never told them what I'd suffered. Well, only Max."

Colin puffed air out. "That was a hard watch."

"It was hard to go through it." Roach smiled sadly. "The doctor was no help because she refused to tell him she had mental issues, just said she was 'sad'. He gave her anti-depressants and sent us on our way. She clearly didn't *want* help."

"Prior to the divorce, what was your marriage like?" Nigel asked. "As in just before she filed."

"She'd got much worse. I woke one night, and she was sitting on me, her hands around my throat again, saying she wished I was dead." She hadn't said or done that at all. "I slept in the spare room after that, locked myself in. I know it sounds ridiculous, but I was scared of her. About a week later, she left. No word as to where she was going. I called around her friends and family, worried about her in case she went off and killed herself. They all said they were sorry we'd split up—that was the first I'd heard of it, but she'd obviously told them. Then the letter came from her solicitor. I didn't see her again until Tesco car park."

"What do you do for a living?"

"I'm a financial consultant."

"So money worries weren't at the root of her behaviour. I can see by this office you're not down on your uppers—the rent must be pretty high."

"I gave her everything she needed. Bought her a car, all that sort of thing. Sadly, it wasn't enough. I can only hope she's found peace now. God, I can't believe she's gone. It's a lot to wrap my head around."

"Are you willing to let us have a look at your bank accounts?"

"Of course. Can I ask why?"

"To rule out you paying someone. You know…"

"Yep, whatever you need, do it." Roach wasn't bothered. His fake company looked good on paper. He paid cash into the bank as if clients had given it to him and sent payments to the taxman. He'd be stupid not to.

Nigel rose. "Okay, bar seeing the CCTV footage from the security desk to show you entering here this morning, we're finished."

"Let me just transfer these two files to an email. If you'd give me your address…"

Nigel supplied it, Colin getting up and going to the window, looking out as if he pondered what he'd seen on the laptop screen. Even if Roach did say it himself, the clips looked pretty damning, painting Alice in a bad light.

"All sent." Roach stood, holding out a hand for them to shake.

Both men did, and he showed them out, closing the door on them and leaning against it. Would his videos be enough to convince them he was abused? Or would they think he had ample motive to kill her, that he'd bided his time, waiting until now to do it? Would the police speak to those two bitches he'd paid off to tell him where Alice had gone once she'd left that flat? Would they tell Nigel and Colin what Alice had told them?

He took his phone out of his pocket. A message had come in from Precious, one he'd ignored earlier, wanting to behave as if he'd been hard at work. He read it, typing in a response.

EVERETT: THEY'VE JUST LEFT. IT WAS ALICE. THE NEWS HAS KNOCKED ME FOR SIX, SO I'M CALLING IT A DAY. MEET AT YOURS?

PRECIOUS: OKAY, SEE YOU THERE.

He collected his laptop, putting it in its bag, and locked the office. On his way to the flat, he mused over the shooting. He purposely hadn't accessed any news sites or social media today in case the coppers took his phone or laptop and saw what he'd been browsing. The less evidence they had on him the better. Yes, he had his burner phones he could have used, but, as sick as it sounded, he wanted to hear about the murder from Precious' mouth, no one else's.

Then he could revel in every gory detail.

Chapter Fifteen

He hadn't seen Granny and Grampy again. Dad said they'd abandoned him just like Mum had. Six years had passed with her rotting in the outhouse, likely a skeleton by now. Everett, who now called himself Roach, no longer cared. He no longer cried over her. She'd deserved all she'd got. His many chats with Dad had made him see the truth, how Mum had goaded him into hitting her, then blaming him for it. But despite their talks, they weren't close by any stretch of the imagination. Roach didn't like the bloke, he was still a bully, although he hadn't hit him since Mum had died. Likely too scared in case Roach opened his mouth and got him right in the shit. With Granny and Grampy going radio silent, not even answering their phones, he reckoned he'd be better off looking out for himself now, seeing as no one else really gave a toss about him. Dad's mum and dad had died before Roach was born.

He walked up the park, hands in his pockets, angry. Dad had fucked off to the Green Dragon again without making any dinner. Roach cooked his own most nights, and *he sorted his packed lunch for school. He also did the washing, basically taking Mum's place. At fourteen, he was well able to live by himself, but the law said otherwise. He planned to get a business up and running, save some cash so he could leave home by the time he was eighteen. Just four more years of Dad, then he could sack him off, never speak to him again. It was best to terminate that part of his life and begin a new one. He'd move away to another area of Cardigan, become someone else.*

He turned into the park, surprised Precious sat on the roundabout with Boycie. She hadn't been hanging around with them much lately, preferring that bitchy gang of girls who thought they owned the school. Still, it was nice to see her, and his stomach flipped, stupid butterflies flickering in his chest. He wished he didn't have a crush on her.

He climbed on the roundabout and sat. Boycie didn't look happy, which wasn't a surprise. The kid hardly ever was lately. He moaned a lot about his mum putting up with his dad hitting her, but at least he had *a mum.*

"What's up?" Roach asked, as if he didn't know. He waited for the sob story to come out, gritting his teeth because it really got on his tits and put him on a downer.

"Mum again." Boycie rubbed his sore-looking eyes. "She's got a broken cheekbone this time. Told the hospital she walked into a wall, the corner of it."

"Blimey." Roach recalled his mother saying something like that to Mrs Watson.

Precious draped an arm around Boycie's shoulder. "Why doesn't she just leave?"

"She's too scared to."

"Then that's her fault for staying," she said. "If you're going to hang around to be hit, what do you expect?"

That was the thing Roach liked about her. She never sprinkled sugar on shit, she told it how it was. And it was true. If Boycie's mum didn't leave, then she must enjoy being given a good hiding. Anything else didn't make sense.

"What d'you mean, she's scared?" Everett asked.

"Dad said he'll find her no matter where she goes. I told her to go to a refuge up north or something, but she doesn't want to leave me behind."

"Then go with her," Precious said.

"Nah, I'd miss you two."

Roach understood that, although back when Mum was going to leave, he'd been more than happy to dump his mates and fuck off with her. But as a teenager, and now he'd spent so many years with these two, yeah, he could understand not wanting to abandon this life for a new one in a strange place.

"Tell her you'll be all right," Precious said. "If she knows that, she might get a clue and save herself."

Boycie tutted. "Don't be nasty about her, Presh. You've got no idea what she's goes through. She doesn't deserve any of it. She's nice, kind, yet he hits her every other day."

"Then hit him yourself," Precious suggested. "Or ring the coppers on him."

Boycie sighed. "I'm scared of him, too, though."

Precious laughed. "Oh, fucking grow a pair."

Roach digested that. So if he told her his father was nasty to him, would she say the same? Grow a pair? She didn't have shitty parents, she had a good life, thanks very much, so she'd never understand their situations. Her father would rather slit his own throat than hit his wife or daughter.

"Until you've lived it, shut up," Roach snapped at her.

"Ooh, get you, Mr Arsey." She got off the roundabout. "And you wonder why I don't hang around with you much anymore. Fuck this, I'm off."

She stalked away, Roach and Boycie staring after her.

"She can be such a cow," Boycie said, "though I can't help but like her."

"Yeah, she hasn't got a clue how other people live." *Roach had come close to telling Boycie where his mother was on several occasions, the knowledge too much of a heavy burden at times. He trusted his friend but not enough to arm him with that kind of information. Boycie would likely ring the police.* "Maybe when you're old enough to leave home and you get a gaff, your mum can live with you."

"Dad would only come round, shouting the odds. Nah, she needs to move right away or she'll end up dead. He'll go too far."

Roach nodded. "Maybe it's like Presh said and she does deserve it, though. I mean, why do shit you're told not to when you know you'll get clouted for it? I don't get it."

Boycie whipped towards him, anger turning his cheeks red. "Don't even think about saying my mum deserves it. You were only little when yours buggered off with that bloke, so you probably can't even remember if she went through shit, but I've seen it all, I remember everything, and she didn't ask for it at all. You're sick in the head if you think it's okay for a man to hit a woman."

Roach shrugged. They'd never agree on this. "Shut up about it then, else we'll fall out. You're as bad as your mum, whinging and moaning yet doing nothing to stop it."

"Go and fuck yourself." Boycie got off the roundabout and stomped away, head bent, hands in pockets.

"Aww, come on, man." Roach chased after him, rugby tackling him to the grass and laughing. "We're like brothers, we can't fall out."

They lay on the ground, staring at the white clouds floating by.

"Dog," Boycie said, pointing to the left.

"Angel," Roach said.

"A baseball bat."

Roach's good mood dissipated. Why hadn't Mum used it to bash Dad's head in? Why had she only gone for his arm? Jesus, she couldn't even get her escape right.

He closed his eyes and imagined her bones. Would her skeleton still be sitting on the toilet, or would it have fallen apart? Many a time he'd had the urge to knock one of the bricks out to shine a torch in and see her. But the thing was, he didn't have the guts. It meant facing up to his part in it, and he didn't want to do that. He preferred to stick to the made-up story that she'd abandoned him. It gained him sympathy whenever he told anyone what had supposedly happened.

He liked that.

※

The papers spilled out of the file onto the floor from the sideboard in the living room when Roach had pulled out one of his school books to do homework. It created a fan, and he lifted it to go and sit on the sofa. Dad was still down the Green Dragon and probably wouldn't be home until after last orders, so there was time to have a look.

He opened the file and straightened the papers. The top one had a typed letter, which had once been folded into four and flattened. There was no address, no date, but he could guess what this was about, why it had been sent to Dad—or, more to the point, Dad had sent it to himself.

> Dear Shaun,
>
> Regarding our last interaction prior to me leaving you. I couldn't explain it at the time, I just needed to get out, and you coming home seeing me with that suitcase, it threw me a bit. But I'm ready to tell you now, and I hope you can understand.
>
> I should never have married you. You're too good for me, and it was a struggle to pretend to be the happy wife when I didn't want to be there. I've been having an affair for three years, and me and him, we agreed to leave together. We both left our children behind. Neither of us wanted them, we just went along with what was expected of us. Call us selfish, I

don't know, but we're much happier with only each other to think about.

I couldn't be who everyone expected, and I'm sorry.

I wish you well and hope you find someone else.

Best, Helen xxx

Well, that was bullshit, but a clever move, nonetheless. Had he posted that to himself after Granny and Grampy had been so he could send them a photocopy? Or was it in case they rang the police and he had something he could produce to show them his wife had up and left, nothing sinister going on?

Roach moved on to the next piece of paper, and his guts went south. A cut-out newspaper article attached with glue.

FATAL ROAD TRAFFIC ACCIDENT

FATALITIES CONFIRMED

A serious head-on collision on Watermere ring road, East London, caused significant delays yesterday with traffic backed up for miles. An unidentified red vehicle cut across the path of a lorry, resulting in a pile-up. Witnesses say the car came out of nowhere and drove off as the first impact hit. One car, a Ford Focus, was crushed between the lorry and an HGV.

The names of the deceased have been released. Stephen Davis, 45. Kevin Linton, 32. Margaret and Gerald Black, both aged 55.

Roach stared at it in shock. The article was dated the Monday after the Sunday Granny and Grampy had gone home. Dad had left shortly after them, saying he needed to nip to the corner shop.

His car was red.

"What the fuck?" Roach muttered.

Could Dad have been involved? If he had, why hadn't he at least told Roach his grandparents had died in a crash? Why lie and make him think they'd abandoned him? What kind of sick bastard was he? And had he been shitting himself all these years, not only worrying that someone might come asking about Mum, but also that the police surely would have come to tell Mum about the crash because they'd have looked up the next of kin.

Had the police been here?

He looked at the next paper, an article from a magazine. Why the fuck was Dad keeping shit like that?

I LIED THROUGHOUT MY MARRIAGE!

Many people won't understand how I could be with someone for years, hating every second of it but pretending everything was okay. I was brought up to find a man, marry, and have children. It was expected of me. It was meant to be my sole purpose, the only thing I wanted to do, and because all of my friends were doing it, I got on with it. Did as I was told.

Throughout the years, I slowly died inside. I smiled, I pretended, and I tried to look after my son as best I could. But it wasn't right, any of it, and one day, when I was at the end of my tether, I walked into a pub and met Frankie. We got talking, and he was in the same situation. Both of us were stuck, desperate for a way out.

We began an affair.

Three years later, we left our spouses and children. I've never been happier. I changed my name and never looked back.

I can finally be myself after years of being forced into a box I didn't fit in.

My advice? Don't do anything you don't want to do in the first place. Don't go ahead and agree just because your family and friends want you to. Listen to your gut. Be happy.

Roach shook his head. Dad must have written this, too. And the worst part? The prize for it was £100. Had he risked putting a cheque in her name in the joint bank account? Had he been using Mum's debit card all this time to withdraw cash so it looked like she was still alive? Was that why the police had never come sniffing round? But with Granny and Grampy killed, there was no one left to report Mum missing…

The enormity of the scam hit Roach, and he stuffed the papers back in the file, not wanting to see more. His dad was a lying fucking arsehole, and the bit he hated the most was he admired him for what he'd done. To get away with all of that…

Dad was a cruel genius.

Chapter Sixteen

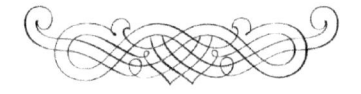

On the way to see Vic, Alice's therapist, Colin groused to himself about being paired up with Nigel. He'd never admit it to her, she might get an even bigger head, but he missed Janine. She'd gone off on maternity leave, only a month left now before her baby made its appearance. He'd been to see her last night under the guise of handing over a big bag of little clothes the team had bought, but really, he'd wanted to gripe about Nigel.

"Sorry, but what do you expect me to do about it?" she'd asked. "I'm not on that team for the foreseeable, and it's not like I have any say in what goes on when I'm not there anyway."

"I know, but it's just... He's a prick."

"You'll get used to him."

"But he's not you."

She'd smiled. "Is that your way of saying you actually like me now?"

"Piss off."

Nigel had transferred from Liverpool, swaggering into the office as if he owned it, upsetting the applecart. No one liked a new senior officer when they had different ways of working, and Colin especially didn't like him because Nigel expected him to actually graft. Janine had taken the lead and basically let him get paid for doing sod all. Yeah, he missed her all right. Maybe he ought to take his retirement early instead of hanging around until the last knockings. Janine would be away for ages, and he wasn't sure how long he could stand spending his days with Nigel.

In the passenger seat, Colin tuned the bloke out. The dickhead was only thinking out loud anyway, going over the interview they'd just had with Everett. God, the shit that man must have put up with if those videos were anything to go by. Colin reckoned Everett must have kept it quiet through shame as well as not wanting anyone to think badly of Alice. As a man, being beaten up by your wife was likely difficult to swallow, and not many would say what was going on at home. Times were changing, though, and more men were coming forward, but how many others were being abused and staying silent?

Everett having the foresight to record Alice in action would help support his innocence regarding her murder, as would the CCTV of his office block. He had indeed entered at around half eleven, his car hadn't moved from the parking area, and no one had left the building via the back. One of the DCs had gone to the Noodle and confirmed a sighting of Everett having breakfast, and another had visited Max who'd said that yes, he'd eaten with him.

He could have paid someone to do it, though.

When they'd got in the car, Nigel had sent Everett's videos to digital forensics then asked Colin to put in a request with the team to look into Everett's business. A quick check at Companies House provided the information—he was a financial consultant, bringing in a hefty wage.

"We'll have to go and speak to her family again," Nigel said. "Not to mention those friends of hers. Why would Alice have told those two about the abuse but no one else? Was that because her family were aware of her alleged mental health issues and would have seen straight through her lies but her friends were oblivious?"

"Maybe. I'm glad he's moved on, Everett. Hopefully, he's found someone a damn sight nicer."

"So you believe Alice abused him?" Nigel asked.

"Don't you? I know we're not meant to say stuff like this these days, but she looked an outright nutter on those videos. She was pissed as a fart in the second one."

"Hmm. It's scary how some people can give a certain impression yet underneath they're nothing like they've portrayed. I mean," Nigel laughed a little, "Everett could be doing just that. Upstanding citizen on the outside, wife beater and cover-up merchant on the inside."

"Digi will be able to tell if he's spliced those videos to show only what he wanted us to see."

"Yep, and if they haven't been tampered with, then we'll have to accept that Alice wasn't the innocent woman we've been told she was—or that he just happened to get lucky with Alice saying what she did and going for him, twice, all while being recorded. A nosebleed and a black eye aren't things to be ignored. She did hit him, that was plain to see, but he could have doctored it, clipping out the bits where he goaded her into such a rage she lunged at him."

Colin didn't want to believe a man could do something so cruel, but he'd been in this job a long time and had seen it all. But Everett didn't strike him as the sort to think the police would be gullible enough not to have those videos picked over, and he'd emailed them to Nigel without batting an eye.

Nigel pulled up outside a house that resembled a cottage, and they got out, approaching the front door. Inside, a receptionist showed them to Vic's office, and the man himself, an elderly gentleman, welcomed them in, going straight to a coffeemaker on the sideboard. Introductions made and drinks poured, they sat on a sofa opposite Vic's comfy-looking chair.

"I have to say I was shocked when you phoned and said Alice was dead." Vic shook his head. "She didn't give me any indication anyone would want to hurt her other than her ex-husband, Everett."

"We've just been to see him," Colin said, jumping in before Nigel could get a word in. "What can you tell us about Alice's state of mind?"

Vic clasped his hands over his belly. "She was at the stage where she felt she'd be ready to move on soon. Away from here. New life, new name, that sort of thing."

Colin frowned. "So she felt she *needed* to change her name?"

"Yes, so Everett didn't find her."

"Weird then, that she kept her married name after the divorce. You'd think she'd want to go back to her maiden name," Nigel said, "erase any connection she had with him. What did she tell you about him?"

Vic listed a litany of abuse, verbal and physical, not to mention instances of gaslighting, where he made out she was the one hitting him. She'd got to the point where she wasn't sure whether Everett was the one telling the truth or if she was. Yes, she'd hit him, in frustration after he'd hit her, and she always, always paid for it afterwards. At one point she'd been confused, unsure of her own reality, which, Vic said, was usual for abuse victims who'd been convinced they were in the wrong.

"When was this?" Colin asked. If the dates matched those of the videos, maybe he'd have to rethink whether Everett had been on the level with them.

"She didn't say. Her mind was jumbled on that score. Everything had become muddled, events leaking into the next and out of order—again, this is usual for someone in her circumstances."

"What was your take on her?" Nigel asked.

"A battered woman desperately trying to save herself."

"Did you get any inkling she was lying to you? That everything she told you was a fabrication?"

"I know she misremembered things occasionally because the next time she told the same story it was slightly different, but I put it down to her memory recall being better on the second or third telling. You have to understand that abused people shut a lot of it out in order to cope. However, once the door's been unlatched, so to speak, information can come out in a big rush or a steady trickle over several sessions. Is there a query as to whether she made all of this up, then?"

"It's something we're looking into, yes." Nigel sipped some coffee. "We've seen evidence that could point to Alice being the abuser."

Vic seemed to digest that. "I've been doing this for a long time, and only one other person has pulled the wool over my eyes to a high degree. He was a sociopath."

"Did you know that when he started coming to see you?"

"No, he presented as anything but."

"So could Alice have been a sociopath? Or a psychopath?"

Vic rested a finger across his chin. "Sociopaths are impulsive and erratic. They find it difficult to keep a job and don't fare well in family life, but they *can* form genuine attachments to people, likely those who are the same as them."

Colin remembered how impulsive Alice had been when she'd gone for her husband. *Were there difficulties with her family but no one was willing to admit to them? Was Everett a sociopath, too, and that's why she'd become attached to him?*

"What about psychopaths?" he asked.

"They're not erratic, they're focused, they plan, work things out to a T. They can meld into family life very well, masking their inner feelings, to the degree that no one would know who they really are. They tend to struggle when it comes to relationships, though—they can play at loving someone, but do they really? After all, a psychopath loves only him or herself, is only interested in what's good for them, what's of benefit. Alice didn't strike me as such."

"If I showed you a video or two…" Nigel took his phone out. "If you could view them, it would help us to know if this was how Alice behaved when with you."

Nigel downloaded the clips then played one. He handed the phone to Vic who sat back to watch. The man couldn't hide his astonishment, his eyebrows rising in places, his lips downturned. During the second one, he appeared shocked at the violence Alice displayed. It ended, and he passed the phone back.

They all drank their coffee while Vic assimilated the visual information.

"I don't know what to say." He pinched his chin. "She didn't show me any tendencies towards violence—in fact, she was dead set against it and couldn't believe she'd hit her husband. I saw she was drunk—that could have played a huge role in her behaviour. We could look at this that she struck him because she was so tired of his abuse, something she's already informed me of. I've already told you she hit him then paid for it later. If we discard what those clips *look* like and turn the coin over, in that *he* was the abuser, do we have a viable situation here where he's engineered it to seem like *she's* the one who's unhinged?"

"It's difficult to tell either way, isn't it." Nigel put his cup down. "So your summary is…?"

"She was abused and just wanted a quiet life."

"Thank you for your time." Nigel stood.

Colin followed him to the door. In the car, he let out a long breath. "I'm all confused now."

"Like we said, digi can verify things, and Alice *could* have been a sociopath. Let's go and see her friends."

Colin put his seat belt on. Maybe he'd go and see Janine later, get her take on this. And that wasn't because he had trouble letting her go *at all*. No, it was for the job, nothing more.

Chapter Seventeen

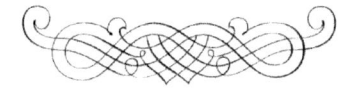

Kayla had ditched her wig and glasses in one of the communal bins, putting them in a carrier bag beneath a load of black sacks. She was Vicky no more, and to be honest, she was relieved. Cooper had fucked off out, hadn't even stayed in to see how this morning had gone or sent a message, and she was a bit hurt by that.

Never mind, he was likely out selling drugs to make enough money for them to go on a little jolly. Spain would be nice.

She jumped at a hard knock on the door. Jesus, was it Everett? He was a dick if he'd come round here. They'd had no contact since she'd messaged him earlier, so perhaps he'd had the police round. She wandered down the hallway, spying two big shapes behind the mottled glass in the front door. Maybe he'd brought Boycie with him.

She opened up and gaped, her stomach bottoming out. "I haven't done anything wrong, I swear. I've got a fella now, and I haven't accused anyone of pinching my arse."

"We're not here about that." George barged past her, Greg following.

She closed the door, panicking. She had to message Cooper so he didn't come home while they were here, but how could she do it without these two asking questions about it? He looked nothing like he had as Parker, but she couldn't risk him walking in, blurting something, then seeing the twins too late.

"I've got to reply to my mate," she said. "She's just asked if I want to go round for dinner. If I don't text back, she'll ring."

They went into the kitchen, and she remained in the hallway, frantically passing on the news to Cooper, telling him not to reply. She deleted the text string then popped the phone inside her bra.

In the kitchen, she went towards the kettle. "Do you want a drink?"

"Not unless it's cold." George leaned against her sink unit, arms folded.

"I've got cans of Coke."

"That'll do."

She opened the fridge and took two out, passing them over, then grabbed her own. Pulling the tab to give herself time to get composed, she sat at the small table with Greg.

"Where's Vicky?" George asked.

Even though she'd told them Vicky had been staying here, now she was Kayla, should she ask how they knew? Would it be weird if she didn't?

"How come you know about her? Have you been keeping tabs on me?" What if they had? Oh God.

George tsked. "Just answer the fucking question."

"She moved out about an hour ago. She's gone back to Essex."

"How do you know her?"

Her stomach rolled over. "I met her in a pub — I think it was yours. We had a laugh, and she said she'd been in some refuge or other, hiding from her boyfriend, but she'd left there and needed somewhere to stay before she went back home. Something about her bloke being caught and being put in the nick? I got the gist she'd grassed him up and needed to wait for him to be arrested before she could leave London. Is she okay?"

"She was when we saw her earlier. Did she ever tell you anything specific about the refuge?"

"No, only that it was some place for battered women."

"What about the people who stayed there? Did she mention them?"

"Nope. I wouldn't have wanted to know anyway — sorry, but if you're going to let yourself be beaten up, you deserve everything you get." Bollocks, had she fucked up by saying that? Yes, she had. As Vicky, she'd heard their views about abused people.

George scowled at her. "You're a nasty piece of work."

Do I look bothered? She drank some Coke to buy time. "Look, she didn't actually say much about anything. She kipped here, and that was it. I hardly saw her because I go to work."

"Yet you're not at work today."

"No, because I've got a day off. You should try it. Having downtime's really good for your mental health and attitude."

George glowered. "Are you taking the piss?"

For a moment, she'd forgotten who she was speaking to, acting like Vicky, minus the disguise and the Essex accent. She had to be Kayla, the woman who was afraid of them. "Sorry, I'm just a bit tetchy today. Time of the month."

"Too much information." George opened his Coke. "Let me get this straight. You barely knew her yet let her stay here. You went to work when she could have been anyone and nicked all your stuff."

"But she didn't. She was nice and just needed a bit of help, that's all. Believe it or not, but I felt sorry for her."

"Have you heard what went on at the salon?"

She frowned. "What salon?"

"Curls and Tongs. Vicky went there this morning."

"No, should I have?"

"What have you been doing today?"

"Dossing about. Did a bit of housework. I was just about to watch Netflix, but then you got here."

"So you haven't left your flat?"

"No."

"What time did Vicky leave this morning?"

"I was asleep so don't know."

"What time did she get back?"

"Again, I don't know, I wasn't clock-watching, but she collected her bags, said thanks, and fucked off."

"One of her friends was shot today. Vicky didn't do it, but she was there when it happened. She didn't mention that when she came in?"

"No! That's a bit weird, isn't it? If my mate was shot, that's the first thing I'd tell someone."

"That's what I thought." George seemed to say it more to himself than anyone. "If she comes back, let us know. We want a word with her."

"Okay."

They walked out, slamming the front door, and Kayla sagged with relief. Fucking hell. They'd now be thinking Vicky was suss because she hadn't mentioned the murder, so all the heat had turned cold regarding Kayla.

She picked up her burner phone and messaged Everett on his to let him know she'd had a visit and what was said. He replied with a thumbs-up, and she dared to chance her arm.

Kayla: Got any more jobs going begging?

His response gave her hope: I'll be in touch.

Chapter Eighteen

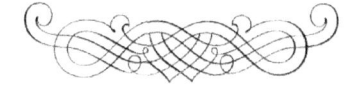

Roach had kind of expected this, although to be fair, when there'd been a knock at the front door, he'd thought it would be the police coming to see Precious. Instead, the twins had stood there, brick shithouses, *telling* him they needed to come in. If it had been anyone else, he'd have told them to fuck off for demanding entry, but with The Brothers, it was best to do as you were told no matter how much you didn't like it. He admired them, the way they handled things, and he likened himself to them. Tough, no-nonsense, get the job done.

They seemed to have squeezed all the space out of the kitchen, what with Roach being a big bloke himself. They leaned against the worktop, Roach standing by the door, propping himself up on the jamb, Precious at the sink, her usual spot.

He was just going to come out with it. The Brothers must know the police would have been in touch with him by now, so what was the point in playing dumb? "Are you here about Alice?"

"You know damn well we are," George snarled, his eyes shooting daggers. "What the fuck's your game, sunshine? What gave you the right to send someone to shoot her? And don't even bother saying it wasn't you, because who else would it be?"

"Hang on a minute…" Roach held a hand up, then realised that might wind the bloke up even more. He lowered it. "I was at the Noodle, then work, it was sod all to do with me. I've not long spoken to the police actually. And before you go in all guns blazing, there's something you should know."

"Enlighten me."

God, this fucker had an attitude problem, but it wasn't like Roach could call him out on it, was it? Not unless he wanted a punch to the throat or worse. "Alice isn't who you think she is. She's a liar."

"*Was* a liar," Greg said.

Roach shrugged. "Yeah, well, it's hard to think of her as dead. I can't get my head around it."

"Why was she a liar?" George clenched his fists. "I'm telling you, if you're fucking us about just to get yourself off the hook…"

"I'm not. I'll show you what I showed the police, then maybe you'll leave me alone. I had nothing to do with her dying. Despite what she did to me, what she continued to tell people I did to her—and you two are obviously included in that—I still cared about her. She needed help but refused to ask for it."

He took his phone out of his pocket and selected the videos from his camera reel. Got the first one up and handed his mobile to George. The twins put their heads together and watched, expressionless. Fuck, they were hard-nosed bastards if they could view that and not show any emotion. Roach thought *he* had his shit under control, but this pair were something else.

Precious, only able to listen, looked across at Roach and frowned. He hadn't told her about the videos, Boycie didn't know either, but it was all coming out now. The question was, did he want Precious to think he'd been a battered husband or should he tell her the truth?

Tell her the truth else she'll see you as weak.

"What are they watching?" she asked.

"I'll explain later. It isn't something I wanted anyone to see, but considering my ex is dead and I could be in the frame for it, I'll put my feelings to one side."

Time seemed to pass slowly, Roach tense. Alice's voice sounded tinny, and he came off as pathetic, a scared man, a pleading man, but then hadn't that been his intention? If the twins swallowed this bollocks, he'd be home and dry.

George gave the phone back then ran his hands over his head, down his face, and clenched them in a double fist at his groin as if to stop himself from punching something. He stared at his brother. It was creepy as eff the way they communicated in silence, a bit like Roach and

Boycie were able to say so much without words. Did *they* look creepy when they did it?

"Why didn't you tell anyone?" George asked quietly. "Why suffer?"

He's taken the bait. "Because she was ill. I didn't want anyone thinking badly of her. I mean, come on, it's obvious she had a problem with violence and drinking. She was always saying it was me when it was her. She actually believed it, too."

"She told us she divorced you for unreasonable behaviour. Why the hell did you put up with that? Why not fight your corner?"

"Because it was easier. And it sounds like you're victim-shaming me, by the way."

George frowned. "That's not how I meant it to come across. I'm just…you're a meaty bloke yet you let a scrap of a thing wallop you."

Greg glared at him. "You sound like Edna. Haven't you learned *anything*?"

The mention of her name almost had Roach jumping in shock. He calmed himself. *Get it together, for fuck's sake.* "Who's Edna?"

"No one." George shook his head. "It seems that despite me watching abuse while growing up, and seeing people who've suffered, I've still got a lot to learn. I'm sorry if I sounded like a wanker, all right?"

Roach nodded. "It's fine, I get it."

"It isn't fine. I've got sympathy for you, I just didn't articulate it well enough."

"Look, my dad brought me up not to hit women," Roach lied. "No matter what Alice did to me, I kept my fists to myself. If she went around telling people I abused her, there wasn't much I could have done to stop it bar going to the police. I chose not to do that. I wanted to help her, fix her. Then she walked out and filed for divorce. I accepted that. The police said she's been spouting nonsense at a refuge where she's been living—why the fuck she was there when we'd been apart for so long, I don't know. Again, nothing I could do about it. I've moved on, put it all behind me. Sadly, because she's dead, it's all coming back, what she did to me. She was sick in the head but didn't deserve to die. Maybe she pissed someone off. Maybe she got into another relationship after me and lied about him, too. I don't know, but I never killed her, nor did I get anyone else to do it. As far as I was concerned, that part of my life was over."

"We owe you another apology," Greg said. "We believed Alice. You were on our kill list, for fuck's sake, then we had to change our plans and put you on the warning list. We were about to come and threaten you to leave her alone, then she got killed."

Roach released a heavy breath. "The coppers said she was shot while she was having her hair done. Did other people see it happen?" He knew they had, Precious had told him everything, but he'd enjoy hearing about it again.

"Yep, and some kid was shot outside. He was videoing the gunman coming out of the salon."

"Poor sod."

"Yeah, we're just about to go round and see his parents now. We visited Alice's family earlier, but they refused our help with the funeral. I got the impression they're not fans of ours."

"It's going to kill them when they find out what Alice was really like. It's bound to come out."

"Can't be helped. So are the police leaving you alone?"

"Seems so, but they said they want to speak to Precious."

"What for?"

"Maybe to check I'm actually seeing her? They've got to build a picture of my life, I suppose. There's not much to see, I'm a boring financial consultant."

"We know, we've had someone watching you. Obviously, we'll pull the surveillance now." George nodded. "Do you by any chance know a woman called Vicky who kipped down the way in one of the other flats? She stayed with a bird called Kayla Barnes."

Roach's hackles went up. Kayla had better not have fucked up. "Nope." He glanced at Precious so she could pipe up with what they'd discussed earlier.

She raised a hand as if at school, then blushed, obviously realising she looked a dick. "I think I might have had a drink with her earlier in the Red Lion. I'd been shopping and nipped in for some lunch. Lil came in, the woman who runs that laundrette, and she said about the shooting. Then Stacey came in from Curls and Tongs, and she had a woman with her. Red hair. Glasses. Lil ended up dragging me over there to talk to them."

"Doesn't surprise me. Lil's a nosy cow. What was Vicky's behaviour like?"

"She seemed a bit dodgy to me. All right, she was likely upset her mate died, but I don't know, there was something about her."

"Lil said the same. Right, we'll leave you be. Sorry again, Everett. We'll see ourselves out."

The twins left, and Roach smiled at Precious, even though he was still angry with her for not following his orders. She'd had one job, to put a few bullets in Alice's *forehead*, but she'd only shot one in the *back* of the head. Now he'd calmed down, he understood she'd had to be quick and hadn't had much choice, but for a moment back there, he'd wanted to beat the shite out of her.

He smirked. "Now they'll go after Vicky, see she's a completely different person, and waste time looking for the one who stayed at Haven. Good luck to them finding her, because Kayla was a fucking demon when it came to pretending to be someone else. She asked me if I've got another job for her. What do you think?"

"She'd do well at the brothel, not that I can see her agreeing to spread her legs." Precious seemed anxious, as if she wasn't sure if she should say what was on her mind.

"Out with it."

She fiddled with her hair. "What were the twins watching?"

"Videos of Alice hitting me, treating me like shit."

"Was that the reason you said about, why you wanted her dead?"

"Yeah, she fought back, got a bit above herself, so I made her pay. She gave me a fucking nosebleed and a black eye. No one walks away from that alive."

Precious chuffed out a laugh. "God, if I didn't know you, you'd scare me."

"I should scare you even though you *do* know me. No one fucks me over and gets away with it."

She reached for the kettle. "Fancy a cuppa?"

"Yeah, go on, then. I could do with a sandwich an' all."

Precious hadn't liked the underlying threat in Roach's words. He'd basically said that she, of all people, wasn't immune when it came to taking any punishments from him, maybe even death. More than ever, she wanted to break free of him, to get that smug smile wiped off his face, but she couldn't do it alone. Now she'd seen him for who he really was, how he'd bump her off if he had a mind, she had to extricate herself from him. The problem was, she lived in one of his flats and worked at the brothel. Dissociating herself from him meant losing her home and her job.

Well, then, she'd have to find a new place and job, wouldn't she.

It was clear to her, seeing as she knew Roach so well, that Alice had been desperate in those videos. She'd likely been sick to the back teeth of being walloped and had struck out at him. He'd all but admitted he'd engineered those videos. He'd made her pay, and all because she'd had the balls to defend herself?

What kind of man is he?
A bastard, that's what.

But Precious was tied to him at the moment, so she'd play along. What else could she do when he was so dangerous? At one point, she'd had the mad urge to blurt out to the twins that she'd been the shooter and Roach had forced her do it, to beg them for their help, but she'd stopped herself just in time. They might not have taken pity on her. They could have dobbed her in to the police.

Prison clothes wouldn't suit her, and God forbid she couldn't get her hair and nails done.

She made Roach's sandwich and took it to the table along with his coffee, wanting to throw it in his face so his skin burned. Maybe now Alice was dead he'd finally find another woman, although since Precious had heard evidence of his abuse towards Alice, she wasn't sure she could keep her mouth shut—but telling the new woman what she was in for would be like signing her own death warrant.

She sat at the table. "What happens to your business if something happened to you?"

He gawped at her. "What the fuck are you asking me *that* for?"

"Just my crazy brain thinking up scenarios. Alice's family might come after you if they think you killed her."

"I doubt it, they're too strait-laced. But I get what you're saying. Don't worry, Boycie's officially down as my partner. He'll take over all the finances and renting the office. I'm leaving everything to him. The house, the flats."

That was good to know, although it hurt her that he hadn't left anything to her. What was she, chopped liver? It just showed how he viewed her.

She'd been in with him since she was a kid, yet her loyalty to him meant nothing. Still, the brothel would continue to run, so she'd have a job, and by the looks of it, she'd have this flat if Boycie let her stay, so if she bided her time, planned things just right, she wouldn't have to worry about Roach anymore.

Sad really, that she had ideas about killing him, but like she'd thought earlier, she was out for herself, and the way he treated her, like some slag he could just fuck whenever he wanted to, well, maybe he needed teaching a lesson.

She found herself wanting to do this for Alice, and it was an alien concept. She'd never been bothered about other people before, especially not their feelings, but Roach really had messed with that woman's mind, and he'd do the same to the next one. It was time she put a stop to it, longstanding friendship or not. If he didn't think highly enough of her to even leave her a few quid in his will, he could go and fuck himself.

"You've got it all sussed, then," she said.

"Yep, everything's in order. But I don't plan on dying until I'm old and wrinkly, so there's no point discussing it."

Someone banged on the door, and she raised her eyebrows at him, hating herself for waiting for permission to answer it.

"It'll be the pigs."

She got up and wandered into the hallway, coaching herself to play another role, one of someone in love with Roach. She opened the door and smiled at the two men on the balcony. "Yes?"

"Precious Granger?"

"Yes..."

"I'm DI Nigel Hampton, and this is DS Colin Broadley. Can we have a word?"

"What about, Alice?"

"Yes, if you wouldn't mind."

"Of course not. Come in. The kettle's not long boiled; do you want a coffee or something?"

"No thanks, we're not staying long." Nigel brushed by her, followed by Colin.

She pointed to the kitchen and waited for them to go in.

"Ah, Mr Sikes," Nigel said.

Precious joined them and leaned against the sink unit. It seemed she was always doing that while listening to men. It pissed her off.

Nigel turned to her. "Just a quick question. How do you know Mr Sikes?"

"Err, he's my boyfriend."

"Right, and how long have you been seeing each other?"

"From a few months after his divorce. We've known each other since school, though."

"Oh, I wasn't aware of that. What are your feelings towards Alice?"

"That she was mentally unstable and needed help. I've seen those videos, and it's clear she wasn't right." She glanced at Roach, as they'd discussed. "Sorry, love, but they need to know about…"

Roach nodded, acting solemn.

"Know what?" Colin asked.

"Everett has nightmares about Alice, even now. He wakes up screaming. She did a number on him, yet everyone thought she was this nice, innocent woman. Because I've been friends with him for years, he confided in me around the time she started hitting him. I told him to go to the police, but he didn't want to. In a way I feel sorry for her. Something was clearly wrong, and maybe she couldn't help being the way she was."

"Did you know her? As in, did you get together with her, seeing as you were friends with her husband?"

"No, she didn't mix much."

"I have to ask," Nigel said, "but where were you this morning between nine and eleven?"

"Shopping," she said and went on to tell them where. "Then I had lunch in the Red Lion."

"We'll check up on CCTV." Nigel nodded to himself. "Okay, we'll be off."

She showed them out, relieved they'd gone. Back in the kitchen, she sat opposite Roach. "That went well."

"You should have been an actress. Makes me wonder whether you've ever lied to me and I just don't know it."

"Bog off." She laughed. "I'm going for a bath, then I need to do my hair for later. I bought a new dress today, so I'll wear it to the Lantern."

"Dressing up for the punters, are we? Are you joining the girls in their profession by any chance?"

"Err, that would be a no." She got up and pecked him on the head, her stomach churning. Her dislike of him had come on quickly, and she'd have to be careful she didn't let it show. He'd be watching her now he'd mentioned her being an actress.

Fucking hell, that was all she needed, him scrutinising her.

In the bath, she thought about all the times he'd done stuff to piss her off, how he'd treated her as less than and she'd taken it. In a way, he'd acted with her like he must have done with Alice, and maybe, as time wore on, he'd raise his hand to her, too. No, he wouldn't dare, would he? She knew too much.

Still, it didn't stop her from worrying about it.

Chapter Nineteen

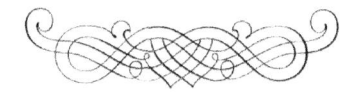

George and Greg sat with Liz and Kenny Feldon in their living room. The couple looked so broken it twisted George's heart. Their son, Ashton, had been thirteen, his whole life ahead of him, then it was snuffed out. How quickly things could change. If he'd actually gone to school, he'd still be alive, and these two wouldn't have tears streaming down their faces and red-raw eyes.

"We had no idea he'd been skiving," Liz said. "Don't get me wrong, he could be a right naughty scrote sometimes, so it didn't surprise me to find out he'd skipped school, but he didn't deserve this."

"No, he didn't," Greg said. "Wrong place, wrong time."

Kenny nodded. "I could strangle the little fucker." He laughed, but it sounded choked. "Not that I would really, I just…"

"We know what you meant." George took a deep breath. "We're looking into this, and we *will* find whoever did it. Hopefully before the police so we can kill the wanker."

Liz stared at him. "Two wrongs don't make a right."

"No, but why should whoever it was be allowed to enjoy their lives when Ashton can't?" George paused at her wince. "Sorry, I can be a bit blunt sometimes, but we're raging about this. We'll string them up and gut them."

"I'd like to see that," Kenny said. "I'd bloody help you do it an' all."

"That's an option."

Liz gasped. "No, it isn't right. Let the police deal with it."

"But they won't get the proper justice." Kenny gripped her hand. "That scum needs to die. Ashton did sod all but video them, and he was killed even though there was nothing that could have identified them."

"Well, if you go down that route, I don't want to know about it, all right?" She dabbed at her face with a tissue. "All I can think about is our boy on a table being cut open."

"Don't torment yourself," Kenny said.

George took a thick envelope out of his jacket pocket and placed it on the table. "For his funeral."

Kenny's bottom lip wobbled. "That's a weight off. We can barely afford shopping these days, let alone a burial."

"Where do you work?"

"The factory."

"Bollocks pay for long hours. Give us a ring when the dust has settled a bit. We'll give you a job."

Liz shook her head. "No, we're not that type—to work for you, I mean. No offence."

"It'll be a legit job," George said. "We've got our eye on another pub. Kenny can run it. There's a two-storey flat above, comes with the position." It wasn't lost on him how a second pub meant he was following in their father's footsteps, but he consoled himself that he wouldn't be like that tosser and snap all of them up. He wasn't *that* greedy. The Noodle had done so well he wanted to replicate it elsewhere. It was a lovely little earner.

Kenny scrubbed at his chin. "I don't know anything about running a pub."

"It's fine, Nessa from the Noodle will train you up. Think about it, eh? Not saying you'd want to move out of here, but sometimes houses hold too many memories after a tragedy."

"I can't even think about that right now," Liz said. "Our child *died* today, for fuck's sake."

"Sorry." It seemed today was the day for George to keep apologising. "Listen, you know where we are if you need us." He stood and took a few less-stuffed envelopes out of his pocket. "This should tide you over while you're off work, what with grieving and everything." He placed them on top of the funeral money and left the house, sucking in a deep breath. He'd always put his foot in it, but fucking hell, once again he'd thought about his own needs over someone else's. Fancy banging on about Kenny being a manager when he had more important shit going on. But he'd wanted to fix things, give them a light at the end of their dark tunnel, he'd just offered that help too soon.

He waited for Greg in the taxi, anticipating a bollocking. His brother got in and drove off, saying nothing.

"Just get it over with," George said.

"You're a fucking knob. A first-class prick. What were you *thinking*?"

George sighed. "I wasn't."

"Hmm, what's new?"

George stared out of the window at the passing scenery. Life went on beyond the glass. There'd be others crying today, having lost their loved ones, too, illness, traffic accidents, all that shit, but the lucky ones got to live another day without grief squeezing their hearts. "Poor bastards."

"I know."

Exasperated, George clenched his teeth. "Who the fuck did it?"

Greg tutted. "If I knew, they'd be dead by now."

"I was thinking out loud, cockwomble."

Greg gripped the steering wheel tighter. "I don't think it's Everett, not after seeing those videos."

"Me neither."

"Or Precious."

"So someone else had a beef with Alice."

"Obviously."

George sighed. "Get rid of that cob on, for fuck's sake. I messed up, I get it. No need to be stroppy with me." He change the subject. "How's Ineke?"

"All right."

"How are things going?"

"All right."

It was clear George wasn't going to get much out of him, so he shut himself up with a sherbet lemon. Everything swirled around in his mind. Vicky had asked Alice if she wanted her hair and nails done. Was that really a friendly gesture, or had it been to get her to the salon so she could be killed? Did *she* know who'd murdered Alice? Was that why she'd fucked off home?

"Go to Essex," he said. "I'll get someone to send me Vicky's address from when we checked her out before when she moved into Haven. I want a word with that woman."

"You and me both."

Greg drove on, his jaw set. Something was bothering him, but George would leave him be for now—*if* he could manage that, which was highly unlikely. Greg would open up eventually, once he'd sifted through whatever it was in his head, but eventually wasn't soon enough. George had a feeling it was about Ineke, but maybe that was wishful thinking. Ever since she'd said shit about George to Greg, George had been in a grump with her. He'd once thought she was the perfect woman for his brother, but now he wasn't so sure.

A sneaky thought entered his mind. What if she'd only pretended to like Greg so she was guaranteed a home and job in London? No, that didn't make sense, they'd offered her sanctuary anyway.

In a bid to get him talking, George asked, "Do you need me to text Ineke to let her know we're going to be late home?"

"No, she knows the score."

Sod this. "Look, what's up?"

"Nothing."

"Yes there is."

"Leave it, will you?"

"Is there trouble in paradise?"

"For fuck's *sake*!" Greg slapped the steering wheel. "We had a row, all right?"

"What about?"

"You."

"Fuck me sideways. When?"

"This morning. She's whinging I spend more time with you than with her."

"She knew that would happen when you two got together. She outright said she didn't mind because she's so busy herself."

"I know, but it seems she's changed her mind—don't they all move the goalposts? She's on about having a kid. I don't want one. Not yet anyway."

"Blimey. Did you tell her that?"

"Of course I did. I'm not going to lie to her about something like that."

"What did she say?"

"She came out with the old chestnut."

"What old chestnut?"

"She said, 'Don't you love me?' I'm not into emotional manipulation, and it felt like that's what she was doing. I don't know how I'm supposed to feel about it. I mean, I fucking like her a lot, you know that, and what she went through in Amsterdam, I feel for her, and I realise she might need some proper stability, me making more of a commitment, but I thought I'd done enough. And we haven't been seeing each other that long. We don't even spend that much time together. I don't *know* her yet, and she doesn't know me."

"If shit doesn't feel right, don't be persuaded into doing something you don't want to do."

"I won't, but it's confused me. I don't think I like her enough yet to move forward, but at the same time I don't want to be another bastard who lets her down."

"You can't stay with her just because of that."

"I know, and that's what I'm wrestling with at the moment."

"Sleep on it, see how you feel tomorrow. Tell her she's moving too fast or whatever. If she's the right one for you, she'll see sense and wait. She *clearly* doesn't know you enough, else she'd be aware that if she pushes, you'll dig your hoofs in and go the other way. Give it time, all right?"

Greg nodded.

"Feel better now?" George asked.

"Yeah."

"You *know* talking helps. Vic taught us that. Maybe go and see him."

"I will once this shit's been sorted." Greg eased round a corner. "Right, we find out who killed Alice, but the question is, was she killed because she's a raving loony and she hurt someone else, or was it a case of mistaken identity? *Was* Vicky the intended mark?"

"I don't know, but we'll soon find out. We'll *make* her talk."

Essex. The place that was split down the middle and a leader ran each side. The invisible central area was called The Line, a metre wide, and if you stood on it, you belonged to no one and bowed to no one. Drug sales, prostitution, and all sorts went on in that long stretch from the bottom-left corner of Rochford to the top of Hinkford, and neither leader could do anything about it. The

Line had been there for decades, put in place by former leaders who'd agreed that no one touched it, nothing happened on it, and it was only there as a clear demarcation between the two sides.

Since those leaders had died and new ones had taken over, a continual war had raged as to who should own it, and arguments broke out under the cover of darkness, gang members shouting at each other from their own sides as if barking over an imaginary fence. George would suggest to each leader that they got together for a meeting like the London leaders did, sort it out that way or, something that made total sense, they split the metre between them and be done with it. But this wasn't his territory, and he doubted the blokes would appreciate him butting in.

Vicky's mum and dad lived on the East Side run by a geezer calling himself Chisel, and he needed a visit first. While George and Greg could have just knocked on the family's door and asked questions, Greg had suggested they go down the proper route, just in case things got lairy.

He parked round the back of the Herringbone, an old-world pub where Chisel had told them to meet him. It had likely been a trio of thatched cottages at one time, the back gardens now the car park and a patio full of tables, chairs, and parasols, customers enjoying their meals and drinks.

The twins got out of the taxi and entered via open French doors, finding a circular, central bar, snooker tables to the left, seating to the right. As promised, Chisel sat ahead on a dais, his white cap easy to spot, the only thing he'd told them to look for as a point of reference. He wasn't a man-sized shed as George had imagined, more the sinewy type, reminding him of Ichabod. Slim but deadly.

They approached, George eyeing the bloke sitting next to Chisel, all brawn and muscles, an ugly bastard if ever there was one. Chisel watched them, nodding to himself, then gestured for them to take a seat opposite.

"Cheers for seeing us," George said.

"Drink?" Chisel asked.

"Unless it would offend you, nah. We want to speak to a certain person then go home."

"Which certain person is this?"

"Vicky Hart from Shaw Street, number nineteen."

"Never heard of her, but that's not a bad thing, it means she's a good girl. What's it in relation to?"

George glanced around at the customers. "I can talk here?"

"Yeah, they know what'll happen if word gets out."

George lowered his voice anyway and told him about Vicky, from her first appearance to her last. When he mentioned Parker Warner, Chisel's eyebrows beetled.

"Now him, I know. He's from the West Side. Gives us no end of trouble. Liked to fuck about on The Line."

"Yeah, we had him looked into. We heard he's in the nick."

"Yep. So this Vicky, she was his girlfriend, you said."

"Yeah."

"I doubt Ria would be pleased to hear about that."

"Who's Ria?"

"His woman. She's just as much trouble as Parker. Sells herself on The Line."

"How long has she been seeing him?"

"Years, mate. Since they were kids, so he must have been seeing Vicky behind Ria's back."

"Is Ria the type to put a hit out on someone?"

Chisel shrugged. "She's involved with some dodgy people, so who knows. You think your shooter popped this Alice instead of Vicky? An accident?"

"It's sounding like it."

"Go and see Vicky. Get answers. I will say, though, that if she needs dealing with, you leave her to me. I'll go and see Ria."

George didn't like the idea of not taking Vicky back to the East End to sort her out if she'd been fucking around with them, but rules were rules. And maybe leaving her to Chisel wasn't so bad. It meant they could go and have dinner at the Noodle then fuck off home. "I'll let you know the score after we've spoken to her."

"And I'll let you know what I get out of Ria."

They said their goodbyes for now and, back in the taxi, Greg inching out of the car park onto the main road, George took a second to get his mind straight. It *was* plausible the hit had been meant for Vicky, and she needed warning that her life might still be in danger.

Greg followed the satnav to Shaw Street and parked outside the house. Semi-detached, grey bricks, black-framed windows. Nice garden. Someone stood at the front window holding a cup, a brunette woman of about fifty.

"Must be the mother." George got out and waited for Greg on the pavement.

They walked up the garden path, the woman frowning at them then disappearing to open the door. She must have put the cup down, because one hand rested on the edge of the door, the other fiddling with a bead necklace.

"Yes?" she said.

"We're here from London. George and Greg Wilkes. Chisel said we'd be okay to nip round."

Her face paled. "Chisel? What the...? We haven't done anything wrong. We're a good family."

He felt for her. She was shitting bricks. "Is Vicky home?"

"Oh God, *she* wouldn't have caused any problems."

"Can we come in?"

"Not being funny, but I don't know you, and if you're the same sort as Chisel, I want nothing to do with it."

"Can we talk to her at the door, then? It'll only take a few seconds to iron something out."

"I'm telling you, my girl will have done sod all." She bit her lip, thinking, then turned to call up the stairs, "Vicky, can you come down here a minute?"

George peered inside. Decent place, obviously well-kept, nothing of the rough-and-gobby Vicky about it. He'd imagined she'd live in a right old dive, but then this was her parents' house so…

Feet and thin bare shins appeared at the top step, growing into a person the farther down she walked. The ends of long blonde hair rested over her chest area, so she must have dyed it from the red. Shorts and a T-shirt weren't exactly unheard of in hot weather, but they certainly weren't Vicky's style. Maybe she'd dressed more demurely for Mummy's benefit.

At the sight of her face, George whipped his head to Greg: *What the actual fuck?* He swivelled his attention back to Vicky who by now had reached the front door. No glasses. No features that resembled their Vicky whatsoever.

"Err, Vicky Hart?" George asked.

"Yes..." She was a pretty, dainty little thing, elfin-like, a wisp that would be blown away with one puff of wind.

"I think we've got a bit of a problem, bruv," Greg said.

D'you think? George gave him a filthy look then smiled at Vicky and her mother. "Um, sorry about this, but I think we've got a case of mistaken identity. You're not the Vicky Hart we know. Just so I can clear something up, do you know a Parker Warner?"

Vicky shook her head, as did her mother.

"You can go back upstairs now," George said. "We'll just have a chat with Mum."

She did as he'd said, a strange ethereal being, her demeanour something he couldn't put his finger on. She was so quiet. So...not really there.

"She's poorly," the mum said. "Has been for two years. Barely leaves the house unless it's to go to see her therapist." She took a deep breath. "Anorexia, although you wouldn't think so now she's put on some weight. So whoever you *thought* she was, she isn't."

"I gathered that." George smiled again. "Unfortunately, it seems her name was used by someone else." A fucking clever move by their

Vicky. "We're sorry to have bothered you." He took an envelope out of his suit pocket and handed it to her.

She held it, staring down. "What's this, one of those leader bribes?" She glanced back up. "We're not people who get involved like that."

"No, it's a gift for your time. Spend it on Vicky."

He walked back down the path, his mind going like the clappers. In the taxi, he stewed until Greg got in. "What the sodding hell's going on?"

"It's obvious, isn't it? Our Vicky picked this Vicky's name in order to get into Haven to make friends with Alice. What we don't know is whether someone sent her there or she's the one with the beef. Our Vicky definitely had an Essex accent, so she's either putting that on or she's from around here. We looked into Alice, and she had no ties with Essex. Our Vicky apparently coming from here might not have anything to do with it. *Did* Alice piss off some other bloke and make out he'd hit her as well, and our Vicky got offended on his behalf—I dunno, maybe she's the fella's sister or something—and she paid for someone to end Alice? Could she have been the bloke's wife?"

A light bulb went off, and George closed his eyes for a second. "There's a parallel."

"To what?"

"Our Edna isn't the real Edna either."

Greg took a deep breath, letting it out slowly. "So someone's chosen other people's names to use so it hides their identities—ordinarily no big deal, happens all the time—but it means our Edna was sent to Haven, too. Edna and Vicky had been keeping an eye on Alice."

"Edna took over the surveillance when Vicky left…" George stared outside at two boys kicking a football to each other across the street. "There's *got* to be a mastermind behind this, one person who sent Edna and Vicky to spy at Haven, unless Edna and Vicky were working together. I still say it isn't Everett."

"Same. But we got fuck all from our check into Alice. She came off as a normal woman, nothing to write home about."

"Someone had a beef with her, though. She wasn't shot for no reason. I'd better get hold of Chisel." George messaged him about what had happened, the reply coming back quickly.

CHISEL: RIA SAID SHE DOESN'T KNOW THIS VICKY, AND I BELIEVE HER. LOOKS LIKE SOMEONE'S PULLED A FAST ONE. GOT TO ADMIRE THEM, HAVEN'T YOU.

GG: YEP. CHEERS FOR YOUR HELP. WE'RE OFF BACK TO LONDON.

CHISEL: ANYTIME.

Greg drove away, and George leaned his head back and closed his eyes again. Someone out there knew all the answers. Someone currently sat there smiling because Alice was dead. None of the current players fitted the bill, so who the fuck was it?

George had a feeling they might never find out.

Chapter Twenty

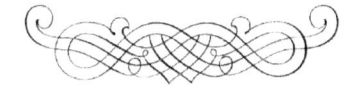

For years, Roach had thought about what Dad had done, how he'd pulled off such a scam and got away with it, all by acting the 'poor me' whenever people mentioned Mum and how she'd just 'fucked off without a by your leave'. Roach had never confronted him about the file, about Granny and Grampy, and took his anger out on the plebs who bought drugs from

him. He'd built a name for himself as Roach, the masked man who could give you the drugs that would send you high as a kite or the punishment that could take you right down a peg or two.

He had power in his corner of the world, albeit it wielded in a disguise, the same as his father, although Dad never spent the majority of his evenings wearing a mask and sunglasses. They were both mean bastards on one hand, nice men on the other.

All he needed now was a decent woman. He'd gone off Precious, his crush withering away. The women he'd met in pubs and whatever hadn't been what he was looking for either. Some of them had been at first, acting all submissive and shit, but farther down the line they'd shown him who they really were, pushy bitches like Precious, all with an agenda to snag his money.

Well, fuck that.

He wanted someone like Mum. He wanted to eventually put holes in her forehead when she dared to try and leave him. He wanted to write a letter to himself from her, saying she'd been having an affair. And he wanted to write a story called I LIED THROUGHOUT MY MARRIAGE! He wanted to recreate the past, to understand it the second time round.

"I'm so fucked up in the head." He laughed to himself and entered yet another pub as Everett, immediately homing on in a woman standing at the bar with her friends.

She glanced across at him, and that spark was there, that frisson of excitement that told him to set off on the chase, to see where it took him. He approached the bar, acting nonchalant, ordering a Bacardi and Coke. A lot of nudging was going on, her friends encouraging her to go over to him, and he waited, glad she was the type who didn't even have the confidence to go after what she wanted.

Someone easily manipulated.

Eventually, she came over and blurted, "Hi, my name's Alice, and my friends would never forgive me if I didn't speak to you."

Maybe, in time, she'd never forgive her friends for pushing her in his direction, but that was a revelation for another day. For now, he'd smile and chat and make her think he was the best thing since sliced bread.

Until he let her see he wasn't.

Chapter Twenty-One

Janine waddled towards the front door. Her dinner sat heavy, and heartburn had paid a nasty visit. She shouldn't have eaten that chicken and mushroom Pukka pie with curry sauce all over it, plus a mountain of chippy chips, but she'd had a craving for them and, knowing she'd suffer later, she'd eaten it anyway.

Her fella, Cameron, was out on a job for the twins, although she didn't know what for. She preferred to keep out of what he did, and now she was on maternity leave and not working for them, she found she quite liked being out of the loop. Being normal, not always thinking about what she had to do for them. No stress. As a workaholic, she'd found it difficult at first, not going into work, but as the days had worn on, she'd got used to it.

Never in a million years had she thought she'd be where she was now, pregnant and happy about it, but ever since the baby had moved, she'd fallen in love with it. Whether she'd take to motherhood was still an unknown, but she'd give it a bloody good try. And she had the brilliant Cameron, the first person to ever love her for exactly who she was.

She steeled herself to face opening the door. Her next-door neighbour had taken to popping round without asking first, and it was getting on Janine's tits. Gone were the days when she'd been free to ignore those living around her, preferring to mind her own business, them not knowing hers. Mind you, she hadn't told Zara, the neighbour, anything much about herself. She had a feeling that if she mentioned she was a copper, the woman would think she could come to her about the couple down the street who kept having loud parties.

The first interaction had occurred a couple of weeks ago. Zara had seen Janine's bump, and that was that. Zara had delivered her third baby three months ago and had taken it upon herself to offer Janine unsolicited advice, much of which Janine already knew because she'd been reading baby books and, grudgingly to begin with, going to antenatal classes. Janine hadn't told her to fuck off yet, but she was close to it.

She took a deep breath and opened the door. Her relief at seeing Colin, even though he'd only nipped round last night, told her how much Zara had been getting to her. Next time she saw her, she was going to have to put her foot down and say she was a hermit or something, an introvert, and she wasn't comfortable with all those visits. She didn't usually have any trouble telling people to piss off, but when it was her neighbour and she had to live near her… A bit awkward, that.

"Sorry, me again," Colin said.

"It's all right, I could do with the company. Come in." She hefted herself to the kitchen, her lower back giving her gyp. She sat at the table, and when Colin came in, she said, "You can make the tea. My feet are swollen."

Colin filled the kettle and flicked it on. "I bet you'll be glad to get that baby out, won't you?"

"Yes, but I'm not looking forward to the process I have to go through *to* get it out. I might be a wimp and go private, get an epidural."

"How the bloody hell can *you* afford to go private?"

She ignored that. "What are you after? Came here to moan about Nigel again, did you?"

"I could do, he's been bugging again today, but no, it's the case we're working. A shooting. Did you hear about it?"

"It was on the news." She'd bet the twins would be going mental, seeing as it was their salon.

She'd wondered whether the hit was meant for them, then dismissed it as the victim had been sitting having her hair done at the time. You couldn't mistake George or Greg for a woman. Still, it could be some kind of warning. As for the lad outside, if he'd just kept his phone in his pocket, he might not have copped it. She touched her belly, guilt poking her for being so blasé about a child's death. If anyone killed hers, she'd lose the plot.

Colin sniffed. "I just needed someone to talk to about it. Nigel likes the sound of his own voice too much, so I don't get many chances to speak. I have to butt in during interviews and whatever to shut him up."

"I'm surprised you even butt in." That was unfair. "Actually, that's not true. You started to get more involved after you'd worked with me for a while."

"I got a taste back for the job, that's why. You helped me see what I'd been doing it for in the first place. Can't say the missus likes it much. She was happier when I hated my job. It meant I scarpered out of the station as early as I could instead of doing overtime." He took cups out of the cupboard and popped teabags in. Stared at the box. "Decaf?"

"I'm pregnant, Colin."

"Oh right. Another new thing to add to the list of 'can't drink and eat while up the duff'. Fucking hell, there won't be anything left that's safe at this rate."

"You get used to it. So, what's bothering you?"

He told her what had gone on so far. The kettle had boiled by the time he'd finished, so he poured water into the cups, steam billowing. "What do you reckon?"

"Those videos. Must have been difficult to watch."

"They were. We're almost desensitised when it comes to violence towards women because it's become *normal*, for want of a better word, so when you see a *bloke* being walloped… I don't mean any disrespect, it's just…"

"I know what you meant. We're not used to violence against men when it comes to a woman being the abuser."

Colin squeezed the teabags and popped them in the bin. "She struck me as unhinged, yet her family and the two friends we spoke to all think she's butter wouldn't melt."

"Isn't that what we find with psychopaths, though? They hide who they are really well, presenting a nice front, when inside they're anything but."

"That's what Alice's therapist said." He added milk, stirred, then carried the cups over, sitting opposite Janine.

"Have the videos been analysed yet?"

"No, sometime tomorrow."

"He could have doctored them."

"Yep, but what if he hasn't?"

"Then you'll have to accept that the information you've been fed about Alice might not be who she really was. Someone killed her for whatever reason, and you've got to work out who and why. Do you think it was the ex-husband?"

"Not really, no. He suffered in those videos."

"What about alibis?"

"Everyone's got one."

"Doesn't mean they didn't pay someone to do it for them."

"Well, if it *was* the ex-husband, he must have got cash from somewhere, because nothing's off with his bank accounts regarding him withdrawing or transferring large amounts in order to pay a hitman. The only weird thing is his cash deposits. No one he does jobs for pays him via transfer."

"Maybe he prefers it that way. He could be on a tax fiddle and only depositing some of the money. People do it all the time. And he could have syphoned off some of the cash from work to pay a hitman."

"Yeah, we'll be asking him about that in the morning." Colin sipped his tea and winced. "Fuck, that was hot."

"When will you learn to blow it?"

"I don't drink tea much, you know that. I'm more of a pop man."

"Well, I haven't got any Pepsi Max, you drank it all last night, so tough shit." She leaned back and circled her ankles. Jesus, they were sore. This was the only baby she was having. The ailments that came with pregnancy weren't fun. "You look naffed off."

"Yeah, I'm at a bit of a crossroads."

"As in…?"

"I might retire now instead of waiting. I don't like Nigel—and I mean I *really* don't like him."

"You probably didn't like me to begin with."

"True."

"Cheeky bastard." She smiled. "So, what, you retire, get bored, and then what? Wish you were back in the job? Wish you had something to do instead of DIY around the house to keep the wife happy?"

"Probably. I feel a bit…rudderless. I need something more. Work isn't as satisfying when you're not there. Nigel hasn't got the same drive.

He's a decent copper, don't get me wrong, but he's not a dog with a bone."

"I've got the perfect thing you could do, but you'd never do it. You're too *good*."

He frowned. "What are you on about?"

She thought about how she'd pulled PC Anaisha Bolton into the twins' fold, how easily the woman had agreed to join the firm, but Anaisha had scores of her own to settle so had jumped at the chance. Colin… He'd already told her he despised bent coppers, and she'd bet if she informed him there was a job going begging now Flint was dead, he'd dob her in. Still, something whispered that she should at least try.

"Forget I said anything." She waited for him to push her for more.

"You've got me intrigued now. What is it? Don't tell me, *gardening*. Bloody hell."

"That's one word for it. It's certainly pulling out the unwanted weeds."

"What?"

"It doesn't matter. You'd hate me if I told you, and weirdly enough, I like it that we've become friends. Sort of. You'd be on the phone to the DCI, and I'd be down the nick in a cell." This was dangerous, she could literally be arrested, but again, something inside told her to give it a go. She reminded herself she had insurance up her sleeve to keep her safe, and if it meant telling him about it, she would. Mentioning the twins would be enough to get him to keep his mouth shut. Wouldn't it? Or was Colin that straight he'd still grass her up?

He eyed her. "You're worrying me now."

"There's a shitload you don't know about me. I'm like the psychopaths we talked about, only showing what I want people to see, when behind the scenes... Look, I'm going to tell you something, and if it goes tits up, I'll deny this conversation took place. And believe me, I can be so convincing, as you'll realise in a minute. I'll worm my way out of whatever charge is levelled at me."

"What have you done, Janine?"

"Let me preface this by telling you what happened to me. All of it." She went on to explain how as a young woman she'd been kept in a basement flat, her captors determined to get her pregnant so they could steal her child then kill her. Then she related her childhood. "So as you can imagine, I left that flat with the determination to put all the bad people away. Only, you and I know, some bad people walk free through lack of evidence, and there's fuck all we can do about it. I became a bit obsessed with making sure they paid for what they'd done, and it meant I eventually went down an alternative route."

"Shit, did you fuck about with evidence and files or something, got them put away on false evidence?"

"Hmm, when I was on my own, yes, but later, I passed information to certain individuals so they could get the justice instead. I worked cases where I deliberately steered things in another direction. There are murdered people who've been murdered because I, and others, wanted them to be."

Colin gaped at her. "Fucking hell… I don't…I shouldn't be here. We'll put it down to baby brain or something, you telling me this. Or you speaking hypothetically. I'll pretend you never told me anything."

"You haven't heard the worst of it yet."

"I don't want to. Honestly, just be quiet. I'm not going to grass you up because I get why you did it, but it was wrong, and…" He sighed. "The only reason I'm keeping my gob shut is because I've grown fond of you, plus you said you doubted you'd be going back as a copper. Trying something else, you told me. Helping people in a different way, so you won't be continuing that shit at the station, and what's done is done, I can't change it, so we'll leave it there, all right?"

"You're a nice bloke. I shouldn't have told you. Sorry about that. But my position is still open…"

"What? You think *I'd* want to do it?"

"It pays well."

"Oh, this just gets worse. You never said you got backhanders for it."

"I just did. Don't you want more money, Col? The freedom to afford a holiday? You've told me loads of times you're sick of working hard with nothing to show for it. All you'd need to do is pass on information, fiddle a few statements."

"No. Seriously, shut up now."

"I got a couple of grand a *week* plus bonuses."

"What?"

"You heard me. Flint took over from me, what with me having the baby, but he was a complete fuck-up, as you know—I had no idea, by the way, that he was a nonce. There's someone else on the books, but she can't interfere in stuff to do with murder, so she isn't really much cop, pardon the pun."

"On the books. Who the fuck were you working for?"

She sensed he was coming round, curious about it rather than gathering information to tell the DCI. That Colin was prepared not to say anything because he was *fond* of her…she should feel guilty about that, but she didn't. If she could get him on board, she'd feel better knowing she'd sent a decent man the twins' way to make up for her mistake in choosing Flint. While they hadn't blamed her for picking a pervert, she sensed they did in private.

"I want you to have a better life," she said. "If you're careful and buy things with the cash you'll receive, never overspending to the point it becomes obvious you're on the take, it works. I've got designer clothes, but if anyone asks, I found them in a charity shop. I kept my car average, nothing flashy, but I own it outright. I have a vanity plate so no one knows it's almost brand-new. As for who I work for… That's the part that might tip you over the edge."

He pressed his fingertips to his forehead. "I joined up to do good things. I can't stand corruption. If I went over to the dark side, I'd be a criminal myself. That's not who I am."

"I'm one, but you still like me. Criminals *can* be nice people, you know."

"I like you because I thought you were on the fucking level!" He drank his tea, staring out of the glass in the back door. "I want to arrest you, but..."

"I know how you're feeling. I'm out of it now, if it makes you feel any better, but I'd still help the individuals in a heartbeat. I hated them at first, I had no choice when it came to working for them, but as time went on, I saw what they were really doing. Removing bad people one at a time, making Cardigan a better place."

He whipped his head round to face her. "Oh fuck, no..."

She smiled. "What?"

"It's them bloody twins, isn't it. Shit, please tell me it's not them."

"The Brothers are like *my* brothers. I love them."

"And they just let you go to have a baby? I mean, didn't you have to do some sort of final job in order to walk away?"

"No. It's not like you think. Yes, they're evil, but they're also lovely. They do some nasty, nasty things, shit I couldn't stomach at first, but once you get to know them, it all changes. You kind of become like them. Weird how that happens." She drank some tea. "Like I said, if you ring this in, I'll deny the lot. You won't win against me. You'll find yourself six feet under. They'll come for you."

Colin shivered. "And will they come for me if I don't take your place? Is that what you've just done, threatened me for them?"

"No, they have no idea I'm talking to you about this." She added the final tidbit. "Cameron works for them, too."

Colin nodded. "Which was why he became your bodyguard. It makes sense now. The Network bollocks…they were protecting you." He shook his head. "This is nuts. I never would have guessed."

"Like I told you, psychopath."

"You're not really one, are you?"

"Fuck knows." She laughed at his shocked expression. "No, I don't think so. I'm just a bit twisted. Maybe my morals are mixed up. Maybe my childhood and what happened to me in that basement skewed my brain. I don't know, but despite sometimes getting frustrated at the twins and what they expected of me, despite wanting to walk away numerous times, dealing with the stress, the worry of being caught, I don't regret it. But I *am* walking away now, I have to become a good person for my kid, so I'll be handing in my resignation at the station at some point. Keep that to yourself, though, will you? I'll be retraining for another career. Probably in sexual abuse, helping the victims."

"It's a lot to take in."

"Do you understand why I did it, though, I mean, *really* understand?"

"Yes." He gulped down some tea. "I don't think I'll take you up on the offer, but I'm glad you trusted me enough to tell me."

"I was selfish by doing it. I want you to take Flint's place. I've got the twins' best interests at heart, and you'd be perfect for them. No one at work would suspect you. Remember, a couple of grand a week."

"That's insane money. What are the bonuses for?"

"This and that. Going the extra mile. But you're not interested, so you don't need to know, do you."

She'd leave it there. He'd come round in the end.

Chapter Twenty-Two

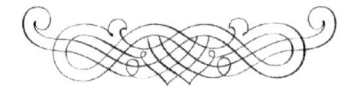

Colin left Janine's an hour later with his head a mess and his heart stretching in two different directions. The policeman in him told him to go to the station and give a statement, but the other side of him couldn't stand to send a pregnant woman to prison, a friend of his, no less. This was *Janine*, the spiky bitch he'd grown to care about, and he didn't want to be the one to whip away her foundations and watch her crumble, not when she'd finally got herself together and found happiness.

That shit about the basement. She had to be a strong person to have come out of that with all her marbles intact. Then again, she'd clearly lost some to have gone in with the twins. Yes, he got it, could see how she'd arrived at her conclusions, but he wished she'd kept her mouth shut. Now he felt like a criminal just knowing about it.

Plus, she had The Brothers on her side. She'd been clever, saying he'd be six feet under, guaranteeing he wouldn't say a word, and he had no doubt she *would* worm her way out of any accusations. She was an expert at disguising her true self. Yes, if he went down the grassing-her-up route there was witness protection, but he doubted very much he'd be offered that. The wife would go mental about it anyway, she wouldn't want to sequester herself away and pretend to be someone new.

But this was massive, what he'd been told, and he struggled to digest it all.

He got in the car and headed home, his mind on the times he'd worked with Janine. She'd tended to wander off at crime scenes to use her phone, and now he came to think about it, she *had* come up with theories that had shifted everyone's attention down another route. He'd just thought she was a genius in how she'd worked things out, when all along she'd been guided by those twins. He didn't like the majority of what she'd said, but the bit he hated the most was when she'd mentioned she'd been forced to work for them. Well, the term she'd used was that she hadn't had any choice, but it was the same bloody thing.

What had they done, chosen her? Had they spied on her to see if she'd be a good fit, then approached? Or had some other copper working for them put her name forward like she'd done for Flint? Who had that previous copper been? He cursed himself for wanting to know, but like the cases he worked, this was a puzzle where he didn't have all the pieces, and he wanted them.

"Fuck it." He pulled over and shut the engine off. Phoned her.

"That didn't take long," she said.

"Don't get cocky. I'm not ringing to say I'm jumping in. Who was the copper before you?"

"Rod Clarke."

"Oh my fucking God!"

"They made him disappear."

"What a surprise. Right, I've got to go. See you when I see you."

He ended the call and resumed his journey, slightly shaky. Why had they had that pleb working for them? Clarke was such a dickhead. He'd seemed to bumble his way through jobs, but maybe that was why he'd been chosen. No one would suspect him. Wasn't that what Janine had said to Colin, too? Did *he* come off as a bumbler? He wasn't sure whether to be offended by that or admire the twins for their clever selection process. Janine wasn't a bumbler, but she'd given off the air she was by the book, so no one had suspected her either.

Maybe that's why she offered me an in with them. People would laugh if my name was put forward as being bent.

He parked in front of his house and took a moment to ask himself whether he'd share this with the missus. Outside of work issues, he hardly kept secrets from her, but this was too big to offload. It wasn't fair to let her carry this burden just so he didn't have to lug it along on his own. She already felt his work life had taken over the one they shared together, a grumble she'd voiced a lot over the past few months. Funny enough, when he'd started enjoying the job again with Janine. Prior to that, when he'd been a lazy bastard intent on getting through the day with minimal effort, she'd been more content.

He got out and walked up the garden path, sticking his key in the lock and turning it. He pushed the door, but it only opened a bit. He pushed again, but something must be stuck behind it. Maybe the umbrella stand had fallen over. The bloody thing had a dodgy leg, something he hadn't had time to fix.

Tutting, he called out, "Can you come and let me in, love?"

She'd been in the back garden when he'd told her he was nipping to see Janine, so she was probably still out there, catching the evening sun. She didn't respond, she likely hadn't heard him, so he poked his head through the gap.

She lay on the hallway floor, arms up by her head, her face turned towards the side of the stairs, eyes staring. Legs wide open, naked on her bottom half. Blood coated the patch between her legs, her knickers around one ankle. Where was the skirt she'd had on? His copper side took over the shock of the husband, and he stepped back, taking his phone out. He dialled the station, speaking to the desk sergeant while elbowing the side gate open and rushing down the path that led to the rear garden.

Washing folded in a basket on the grass. A mug on the patio table, her coffee gone. The back door open. A smear of blood on the lino just beyond the edge of the bristly mat. Her skirt in a heap by the fridge. Oh God, had the bastard started on her there, managing to get the skirt off, then she'd run towards the front door but he'd caught up with her? Had she screamed?

He related everything he saw to the sergeant, because if he was talking, he wouldn't have to think, *really* think about his wife, clearly dead, clearly raped. He wouldn't have to think about what she'd gone through, how she'd have panicked, perhaps cursing him because he'd bloody well gone to Janine's *again* instead of staying home, work more important than her, as usual, and if he'd been there, the rapist wouldn't have risked attacking her.

"Can you go and check for signs of life, Col? I know it's hard because of who she is, but…"

He swallowed. "Yeah." Inside, he stepped over the red smear and walked into the hallway. Crouched and reached a hand out to place his fingers on her neck. "Nothing."

"Try CPR, please."

Colin placed his phone on the radiator cover and got into position. He tuned out the fact this was his wife; the only way he'd get through this was by pretending she was another victim, someone he didn't love. Someone he hadn't envisaged sitting beside him in old age.

He counted out the compressions. Breathed into her mouth. Repeat, repeat. It seemed to go on forever, but he knew how this worked. If she wasn't breathing by now, she never would.

He stopped, for her, because she wouldn't want him putting himself through this torment. He picked up his phone. "She's gone. She's still warm. She would be anyway, because I wasn't gone long. An hour and a half, max."

"Where did you go?

"To see Janine Sheldon. Her baby's due in a month." Why had he said that when the sergeant already knew? *Stupid prick.*

"I'm sorry, mate. Go out the front."

Colin cut the call. Couldn't stand to hear another sorry. His bottom lip wobbled, and he told himself to remain calm. He made his way out of the house and waited on the pavement, his back to the property. A neighbour over the road came out and paused halfway down her path at his raised hand.

"What's happened?" she asked.

He got himself together. "Did you see anyone here after I left?" She'd seen him pull away from the kerb, and he'd called her a nosy cow under his breath. She was always watching. "Please tell me you did."

"I didn't, sorry…"

Typical. The one time he needed her to spy, and she hadn't.

He kept grief at bay, not wanting to face what had happened. The word *justice* blared in his head, and he finally understood Janine.

Prison wasn't good enough for the man who'd done this.

Only death would suffice.

He dialled her number.

Chapter Twenty-Three

Precious, in her new dress, sat with Goddess in the living room at the Lantern. The new woman had come in to watch how things worked before she started her first shift tomorrow. They'd been chatting, Precious getting to know her, wishing she had the same aura as her—if it was a colour it'd be golden.

Goddess had grown up in Bermondsey with nice parents who'd unfortunately died a couple of years ago in a car crash. She'd gone off the rails a bit, snorting coke to get through the thick wall of grief, offering sex to fund the habit. She'd got herself clean six months later and joined an escort agency but had found the work bland as no extras were on offer. She needed sex in order to feel anything, and she'd admitted she pretended the men loved her, even if only for the short span of time they were together.

Shame.

Precious had given her the work spiel already, and Goddess had got the gist—the men came into the living room to wait their turn, Precious flirting with them to get them all spiced up, then they disappeared into one of the bedrooms. Precious had taken Goddess into the room she'd use, showing her the goods hidden out of sight in the wardrobe, condoms and the like. She could hang her outfits up in there, and Widow ensured they were cleaned ready for the next shift.

Boycie popped his head around the door. "All right?"

Precious smiled. "Yep, you?"

"Can we have a quick chat?"

Precious looked at Goddess. "Do you think you can do my job for a bit?"

Goddess nodded.

Precious left her to sweet talk the men, following Boycie into the office at the back. He closed the door, and she sat at the desk. Widow usually worked in here, but it was her night off.

"What's up?" she asked.

"Roach has gone off his nut."

She tensed. "What do you mean?"

"He rang me, asked me to go round his gaff because he snorted too much powder and couldn't see straight. He panicked and got hold of me."

Precious held her smile back. This was fucking perfect. If fate was real, she was on Precious' side tonight. "What do you think's happened, he regretted having Alice killed?"

"No, he was celebrating and got carried away. It's not the first time he's done it either. I'm worried about him."

"What, that he might do himself some damage or he'll become a liability?"

"A liability. I'm the one who runs everything really, did you know that?"

"No…"

"He comes out on the streets with me, acts the hardman with his face covered up, but it's me who's into the nuts and bolts, he just parades around lapping up the fear from the poor cunts he scares the shit out of."

"Poor cunts? I thought you were just as bad as him when it came to beating people up."

"When they deserve it, yeah, but he's done over a few who haven't done fuck all."

That was news to her, as was Roach overindulging in the white stuff. "Did you say anything to him?"

"What, and get barked at? No thanks."

Fuck it. She dived in. "I'm sick of him lately anyway. He treats me like shit. 'Open your legs, Precious. Suck my dick, Precious.' I'm nothing but free sex to him. I want something more, know what I mean? A proper bloke, one I come home to. I'll never get that as long as he keeps using me. I'm hoping now Alice is dead, he'll piss off and find someone else." She ploughed on. "And that's bothering me an' all. What if he beats a new woman up, too?"

"I know what you mean. He wasn't nice to Alice, I saw it for myself. You've seen me trying to stop him from having her killed. He wasn't having any of it."

"Did you step in and save her, though? No, you left her to it."

"I couldn't. You know what he's like."

"Unfortunately, I do, but you could have got her to a safe place if it bothered you that much. How long's he been on the sniff?"

"A long while. Years."

Why didn't I know about this? Yet again, this was proof she wasn't really part of their trio. "That must be what's changed his personality, then, because at one time we could have brought this shit up with him, made him see he was being an arsehole. These days? Not a chance. Have you seen the videos?"

Boycie frowned. "What videos?"

"The twins popped round, and he showed them. I didn't see, but I heard. Alice sounded a right nutter, and he said she'd hit him. I don't doubt it, not by George's reaction, but Roach was making out he was the victim, but we both know he wasn't. He all but told me he'd set Alice up by recording her—as luck would have it, what he'd taped makes her look like an abuser. I knew he was sick, but seriously? Why the hell is he like that?"

"He blames his childhood yet won't talk to me about it."

"I don't like who he's become. I'm sick of being treated like shit. I'm thinking of getting out."

Boycie seemed alarmed. "Where will you go?"

"I don't know. I wish he'd just drop dead so I wouldn't have to worry about it." She laughed as if she'd been joking.

"It'd certainly solve a few problems."

He laughed, too, but they stared at each other, understanding passing between them, or was that her imagination?

She leaned back and folded her arms. "If you think about it, he's always been an arsehole, always told us what to do. We've both killed for him, but it was expected, and he didn't show any appreciation. When I told him earlier about how the shooting had gone, he didn't say thanks or anything, just had a go at me because I didn't put bullets in her forehead. Why did it need to be so specific?"

"You did offer your services, though, so expecting appreciation is a bit much."

"I know, but he could at least be fucking grateful. He annoyed me, too. I went up for a bath, and he waited until I'd got dried and did my hair, then he forced himself on me."

"He raped you?"

"I didn't say no, but…look, I didn't want to do it, all right? Anyway, how's things been left with him?"

"He passed out, so I put him in bed."

I hope he dies in his sleep. "I spoke to him about the business today. He said you're down as his partner and he's left everything to you. Is that true?"

"The partner bit is, but I didn't know about him leaving me shit. What about you?"

"He never said, so I assume I get fuck all. I mean, I've given him my life since I was eighteen, and that's all the thanks I get for it? Honestly, he can go and do one. He doesn't deserve either of us."

"Can I tell you something?"

"Err, duh. I've just told you stuff that could get me right in the shit if you went back and told him, so what do you think?"

He sat on a chair in the corner. "I've been thinking about getting out, too."

Blimey, she hadn't expected that.

"It's all very well," he went on, "doing what we do, but one day we'll get caught. I can't stop thinking about it. We're not kids anymore, we need to grow up. Someone's bound to set us up, a drug user probably, and they'll go running to the twins. I keep panicking about a sting operation where they catch us." He paused to stare at her smiling behind her hand. "Don't laugh, I'm being serious."

"Sorry."

"The Brothers could ambush us when we're out there roughing people up. I keep telling Roach to go to them, tell them what he's doing and offer to pay protection money, but he refused. Now Alice is dead and they'll be involved, that avenue's closed. How they haven't cottoned on to what we've been up to I'll never know."

"Because Roach is scary enough to prevent people from even *thinking* about grassing him up. And no one knows what he looks like, so he can't even be identified. Thankfully, neither can you."

"And there's this place, direct competition to the massage parlour at The Angel. There's the drug sales, all the other crap we get up to. Jesus, it's all getting to me. Then there's you."

"I'm okay because as far as anyone's aware, I'm just a woman who chats men up in a brothel. All right, I'm linked to him as Everett, but no one knows he's Roach, so it's fine. *You've* got your actual name down as being his bloody partner."

"That side of it's okay. I'm a silent partner in the financial consultant business. If the police look into it, all they're going to find that's off is the cash deposits in the bank, not transfers."

"So say they have to poke into all that to clear him as a suspect, will they want to speak to the fake clients and look at *their* bank statements to see if they've withdrawn cash that matches what he put into his account?"

"Fuck's sake."

"See? He isn't as clever as he thinks. We're better off getting out while the going's good." She had a thought. "What about the motorbike and the gear? What's happened to it?"

"I set fire to it myself. I wouldn't want you getting in the shit because of DNA or whatever on the clothing."

"Thanks, at least *you* care about me, which is more than I can say for him."

"I've always cared about you, except you didn't notice."

"What?"

He laughed, the sound unsteady. "I've fancied you forever, mate. Christ."

She recalled the conversation at the kitchen table.

"Don't even think about it until I'm done."

"Yep, but when you are, it's fair game."

"You were talking about me, weren't you?" she said. "The 'fair game' comment."

Boycie nodded. "I was letting him know it had to stop, him using you. He knows how I feel about you, which is why I think he fucks about with you. He staked a claim so I had no chance. I was just getting it out there that I was going to let you know how I feel, not that you'd even have me, but whatever."

"You should have said…"

"You were blinded by him."

They sat quietly, Boycie staring at his twiddling fingers in his lap, Precious' gaze blurring. How could she have been so stupid as to not see? Boycie was kind, he wasn't arrogant, and he always made sure she was all right.

I thought he saw me as a sister.

"I imagined killing him earlier," she whispered.

Boycie scoffed. "Fuck off!" He looked over at her. "Shit, you're serious."

"For Alice. You know, get her some vengeance. I don't know why I even care about her now. I didn't give a toss before. Him being dead is the only way I can get away from him as well as keep my job and the flat—providing you'd let me stay there, that is."

"Of course I bloody would." He shuffled forward to sit on the edge of the chair and propped his elbows on his knees. Cupping his face, he sighed. "Killing him is a bit steep, Presh. He's our mate."

"I know, but unless you can convince him to give all this up or approach the twins about what he's doing, then we're stuck and risk going down with him. Like you said, he's going to get caught one day."

"There must be another way."

"There is, but you won't like it."

He dropped his hands so they dangled between his open knees. "What…"

"We take a walk to the other side and grass him up to The Brothers."

Chapter Twenty-Four

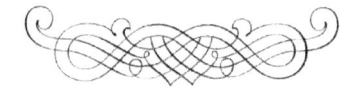

Roach had been watching Alice since she'd had the audacity to leave him. She'd gone without saying a word. While that was going exactly as Roach had envisaged, he still struggled with the fact she'd fucked off, even though he'd wanted her to. It was one thing to want it, another for her to actually do it.

In his fantasy world, Mum really had left of her own free will; she wasn't dead in the outhouse, still, after all these years. In his head she'd walked out, the same as Dad's story to all the neighbours, leaving behind her little son who'd waited in vain for her to turn up in the playground, only to feel lost and alone when she hadn't. It had been easier, back then and now, to follow that tale, to be pitied, patted on the back as a 'poor thing' who 'didn't deserve to be abandoned'.

Wasn't it weird, that even though Roach had walked out of the family home at eighteen and hadn't looked back, how he hadn't spoken to his father in all that time, he still maintained the charade. Was it some kind of latent guilt, that he'd helped to brick her up and hide her from the world? Did the boy he'd been still live inside him, buried beneath the nasty cunt he'd become, desperate to tell the truth?

He didn't understand himself and wouldn't bother trying to. It hurt too much, took too much work. He embraced all of his weirdness, the traits he'd clearly inherited from his father, and just accepted he wanted to kill Alice and watch the fallout: Mum's death recreated but seeing it from an adult's perspective.

Sometimes, if he spotted Dad in the Green Dragon whenever he walked past, Roach went to his father's back garden and braced a hand on the outhouse, beside the newer bricks. He spoke to her, cursing the bitch for leaving him — however he looked at it, she'd still left him, even though Dad had killed her. She'd still made some kind of decision that had led to him doing that. It was still her fault.

He paused outside the Green Dragon now. Dad sat at his usual table near the bar with his cronies, the four old men together, putting the world to rights — a world that had changed far beyond the one they'd recognised as thirty-somethings. All of their wives had snuffed it, although he doubted any knew Mum was dead. Knowing Dad, he'd probably taken that magazine article into the pub and flashed it about for all to see, moaning that she was making money out of leaving him, and wasn't it a piss-take to tell all and sundry that basically, she'd never loved him? "Ah, fuck the auld bitch," Mick Berry would say, then the night would continue, their wives forgotten, a new topic discussed.

Roach didn't want to end up like them.

He walked on, past the pub and towards the block of flats where Alice now lived. He'd already driven past and checked for any CCTV. Only one first-floor flat had a video doorbell, which didn't surprise him. People around here weren't exactly rolling in it, most of them plebs on benefits.

He climbed the concrete stairs, a couple of steps drenched in fresh piss, the smell of dried urine strong. Why did some people have a slash outside? Why not go to the loo? He didn't get it.

He moved higher until he reached the second floor. She lived in number sixteen, halfway down the balcony, which could prove a pest if she screamed—he doubted he'd reach the stairs in time before someone come out and spotted him. Still, he'd decided on the soft approach, fooling her into thinking he was sorry, then lashing out.

He stopped in front of her door. A net curtain gave her some privacy along with the leaf pattern on the glass, and there was a peephole. He glanced to the side at a window with a pink blind down, the inner sill covered in tiles so likely the kitchen. He suspected the stairs would be to the left, the living room down the end of the hallway along with any bedrooms and the bathroom.

He knocked. Waited.

A light snapped on inside. Someone approached, their shape growing bigger the closer they got. The door inched open, prevented from going too far by a silver chain halfway down. She peered out at him, her eyes going wide, then she went to slam the door in his face. He held his hand out to block it.

"Please, can we talk? I can't stop thinking about what I did to you. Can I at least say sorry?"

She eyed him, wary, then the chain tinkled where she'd unlatched it. She was an absolute fool, being prepared to let him in. The door moved wider, and she backed up a little, hands at her throat. He entered and smiled. Shut the door.

"Are you really *that dim, Alice?"*

His fist shot out and connected with her jaw.

Chapter Twenty-Five

Roach had a banging headache. He woke to sunlight streaming into his bedroom, vaguely recalling Boycie helping him to bed last night. Annoyed the fucker hadn't thought to close the curtains, he got up, his mouth dry as a nun's chuff, and chugged water from the bathroom tap. A shower washed away the clamminess on his skin, but he still felt like he'd sniffed more than he should have, which he absolutely had. But he'd been so fucking *pleased* about how the day had gone: Alice dead; the police and The Brothers believing those videos; having sex with Precious before she'd gone to work. He'd got away with murder, and unless they'd fucked up somewhere and the police caught wind of it, he was home and dry. Poor pathetic Everett, abused husband.

He dressed, going down to the living room in search of his phones. They lay on the coffee table, and he picked the work burner up, the screen coming to life. 11:49. Fucking hell, he'd slept the morning away. He dialled Boycie for an update on work matters (there was a drug delivery this morning), but he wasn't answering. It clicked over to voicemail.

"Ring me as soon as you hear this," he barked, then tried Precious. The same thing happened, but that didn't surprise him. She worked into the early hours so may well still be in bed. Her voicemail message came on, and he waited for the beep. "If you see Boycie, tell him to give me a bell."

He went to the kitchen, put his phone on the side, and shoved some bacon in the microwave, turning the dial to four minutes. He buttered bread, pissed off that it was too cold so ripped the slice. He tried again, with spreadable margarine this time, and some irritation left him at it gliding over nicely. Little things got to him more than they should.

Sandwich made, brown sauce squirted on the bacon, he sat with a Diet Coke at the kitchen island and ate. Where was Boycie? Why hadn't he used his key to come and check on him? Then again, maybe he had and Roach was out for the count. He laughed. Boycie knew better than to wake him up if it wasn't an emergency.

He ate the last bite and pushed the plate away. Closed his eyes and sank into the feeling of no more Alice. Yes, he expected another visit from the police or for them to ask him to go to the station—they had his bank account to look through, and they were bound to ask about the cash deposits. Boycie had sorted that years ago, he had people who'd say they'd had a consultation with Everett, then the coppers could fuck off and set their sights elsewhere. It wasn't a crime to only take cash from clients.

Tonight, he'd go on the prowl. Look for someone else to shag. To torment. He'd play the long game, catching her eye then dating her for a bit. Fucking Precious in the meantime, because blue balls weren't his cup of tea.

Talking of Precious… She hadn't seemed herself last night. A bit stiff, none of her usual enthusiasm. And that chat they'd had in the kitchen before her bath. She'd asked about the business. What the fuck did it have to do with *her*? He'd remained calm about it, but bloody hell. Was she fishing to see if he'd left her anything in his will? She always had been a greedy tart, her eyes on the money. How could he explain to her that although all three of them had been friends for years, Boycie was his best one? The only person Roach trusted one hundred percent? She wouldn't understand, so he'd never tried explaining it to her.

Was Boycie all right? Had *he* been acting funny lately? Nah, he was just the same, although he had expressed his worries over someone running to The Brothers about them eventually. Boycie tended to do that, fret, get something in his head that swirled around until he went mental with it. An overthinker. They hadn't been caught yet, and

Roach doubted they would be. People wouldn't dare set him up.

He rang the Lantern, just in case Precious had a daytime shift and he'd forgotten. Widow answered in her usual sultry way, then cut the crap once she realised it was him. The refined accent switched to East End in an instant.

"All right, boss. How's it diddling?"

"Everything's fine. Is Precious in today?"

"No, tonight."

"Right. How's the newbie doing?"

"She's perfect. She's here now, actually. Her first shift's tonight, but she's here to try on outfits. Maybe you should come and meet her. We haven't seen you for ages."

"Been busy."

While he'd known the twins' men had been observing him, he'd acted as Everett, going to the fake financial office, then home or to see Precious. As The Brothers had called off their dogs, if he wasn't worried about the police watching him, he'd have returned to his Roach duties, but for now, it was best he played it safe and left shit to Boycie.

"I'll come by soon, all right?" he said.

"No worries, you know you can leave this place to me."

"Yep." He cut the call, jolting at the doorbell pealing. It wouldn't be Boycie, he'd use the key, so it might be the police. He walked to the front door, opening it to find Max's wife on the step. "Oh, hello."

"We heard the terrible news." She held up a glass dish of lasagne covered in clingfilm.

He almost burst out laughing. "Oh, you're too kind." He took it from her, the glass still warm from where she must have made it this morning. "Yes, it's awful. Alice was so troubled, but she didn't deserve this."

"Troubled?"

"It'll probably come out in the papers, so you may as well know. She had issues with her mental health and alcohol. She used to hit me."

"Oh my God! Alice?"

"I know, difficult to believe, but I have video proof of her attacking me. The police have it."

"That's just…oh, you poor thing. Max asked me to pop round. He did knock earlier this morning before work but got no answer. He wanted you to know the police had asked him for your alibi yesterday. Of course, he told them you went for breakfast. I don't understand how they could possibly think it's you anyway."

"They're just doing their jobs." *You can fuck off now, love.*

"Will you be okay? I mean, I know you were divorced and everything, but it still must have come as a shock."

"I'll get by. Thanks for this." He lifted the dish.

"I'd best get back. I left beef wellington in the oven. If you need anything…"

"I'll ask you, yep."

She walked off, and he closed the door. The silly cow had made lasagne based on him telling her last time it was his favourite. Nice of her to have remembered, but fucking hell, talk about stalker tendencies. He dumped the dish in the fridge and wanted to scream at yet another knock on the door. He stomped towards it, reminding himself to be calm, to be Everett.

He opened it, Nigel and Colin standing there.

"Afternoon," Nigel said. "We did pop to your office, but the security guard said you weren't in."

"I took the day off. Alice, you know…"

"Understandable. Can we just come in for a minute to ask a couple of questions about your bank statements?"

He stepped back, let them in, and shut the door. In the living room, he spied his personal phone and thought about his burner in the kitchen. If that went off and they asked why he had two mobiles…

"Would you like a drink?"

"Got anything cold?" Colin asked.

"Diet Coke?"

"Lovely."

Roach went to get it, switching the burner off and shoving it in a drawer. He returned to the living room, handed the cans over, and sat on the armchair. The coppers lowered to the sofa.

"What can I help you with?"

Nigel opened his can. Sipped. "Cash deposits. Any reason for those? Most clients would pay via transfer or one of those handheld payment machines, surely."

"I work on a cash-only basis and wouldn't even use a bank if I didn't have to show proof to the taxman." He smiled. "Cards and electronic banking has taken over, and I'm of a mind that having notes in my hand makes me actually *see* what I've earned instead of staring at numbers on a screen. It helps push me to earn more. Call me weird, but that's all it is. A tool to help me climb the ladder. I have all my clients' names in a file if you want to see them, and you can certainly go and ask them if they paid me in cash. But there are also scans of the receipts I've given them. I expect they've kept them for tax purposes so you can match them up."

"You visit the bank every day to deposit what you've been paid."

"Yes…"

"Some days it's a few hundred, others it's thousands."

"Yes… Sorry, I don't understand what you're getting at."

"Is it not just a flat fee for what you do?"

"Um, no. Some people need several appointments in order for me to deal with their finances. Then there's the work I do for them to ensure I invest it in the right places or they're spending it effectively."

"I see."

"Is that all you needed me for?"

"Yes."

"Are there any developments?"

"The videos were analysed this morning. We had to check whether they were genuine. I'm pleased to say they are."

"Right, so what happens next?"

"We'll be in touch with anything significant, providing you want to know. As she's your ex-wife, and given the abuse, I can understand if you'd rather not."

"No, please tell me. Like I already said, I still cared about her."

Colin popped his can tab and guzzled. "Your alibi checked out."

"Right."

"Do you ever keep some of the cash back?" Colin asked.

"What are you suggesting, that I'm not being honest about my earnings?"

"Many people do it. It would then be easy to save some in a box until you had enough to pay a hitman."

"Colin!" Nigel glared at him.

"Hypothetically," Colin said.

The coppers stood.

"We'll be off, then." Nigel held up his Coke. "Thanks for the drink."

Roach saw them out, closing the door and going to the kitchen to get the burner back out. He turned it on, expecting to see a notification that Boycie had phoned or messaged, but there was nothing.

What the fuck was going on?

Chapter Twenty-Six

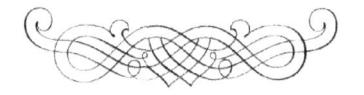

Precious and Boycie sat in a room in the parlour at The Angel. They'd agreed to tell all, and now they were opposite the twins, she wondered if Boycie was having second thoughts again. He'd struggled with the 'Roach is my best mate' thing, but ultimately, being free of him had won out.

Yes, Boycie was definitely out for himself, and she'd worried he'd dob her in, too, but his confession that he loved her, wanted her as a wife... Could that be a trick? Was he going to turn her over to the twins during this meeting? If he did, she'd wheedle her way out of it somehow, but the prospect of it had her uneasy.

She'd trust him. For now.

Despite him swinging from guilt to greed several times last night, he'd settled on greed. They'd come up with the bullshit needed to keep themselves out of the hot seat and put Roach firmly in it, they just had to hope The Brothers believed them—and that they could act innocently enough to pull this off. For this little episode, they'd only know Roach as Everett.

She was safe—she never dealt with the drug people, and they had no clue who she was. Boycie was safe—he'd always worn a mask when with Roach, his hood up and sunglasses on. As for their work burner phones, they'd turned them off and ditched them. If the twins found Roach's it didn't matter, because they'd all used code names.

There were so many unknowns with this, and the twins weren't stupid. If Everett was interrogated, he'd likely drop them in it. They might believe him instead. He was so good as Everett, at appearing calm and *normal*. None of his neighbours would believe he was a wanker.

"What's going on?" George asked, looking straight at her.

Her stomach flipped over. She didn't like his stare, it seemed to say he knew too much, like his assessment of her told him all he needed to know. "We thought you ought to know what we've found out."

"What's that, then?" He swung his attention to Boycie.

Her friend shook his head as if he still couldn't accept what had happened. She'd always known he was a good actor, and it further fuelled her worries that he'd switch this around on her and convince George and Greg that she was in on it all with Roach.

Boycie scratched his nose. "I can't fucking believe it. We've been mates with Everett since we were kids, and the shit I found on his laptop last night…"

"What shit?"

"Let me just say we had no fucking clue, all right? As far as we're concerned, he runs a financial business and a brothel, nothing more."

Greg folded his arms and cocked an eyebrow at her. "A brothel?"

Precious wanted to take a deep breath before she dived in, but would that make her look suspicious? "Yeah, I thought you knew about it. It's a house, the Orange Lantern. A woman called Widow runs it. She won't have a clue who Everett is because he's weird and wears a mask and sunglasses whenever he's there. He told me he couldn't afford for any of his neighbours to see him if they went there for a bit of how's your father, that's why he disguised himself."

"Right…" Greg sat forward. "This is the first we've heard of a knocking shop."

"What?" she said. "You *didn't* know?" She glanced at Boycie. "He told us they did."

Boycie gritted his teeth. "Bastard."

"So is that it?" George asked. "He runs girls without permission?"

"I wish it was." Boycie sighed. "Last night, he rang me, saying he'd done too much sniff. He's been caning it lately. He'd got paranoid, didn't feel well, and panicked. I went over to his gaff—

I've got a key—and he was fucked off his face. His laptop was open on the coffee table, coke dust next to it. There was an Excel spreadsheet on the screen, one I hadn't seen before. Anyway, I got him up to bed then went down to see what it was. I'm the one who sorts his shit for the financial business, you know, I get his accounts in order—but that's all I do, okay? I've got fuck all to do with the brothel other than I go there and deliver stuff to Widow or whatever when he's busy."

"What kind of stuff?"

"Condoms, lube, shit like that. He told me to disguise myself, too. I didn't understand it, but I did it."

"I get the feeling there's more to this," George said.

Boycie linked his fingers. "Yeah. The spreadsheet was for drugs. Like, who bought it, how much they had. A client list. I minimised the window, wanting to see if it was in a folder, and it was. Fucking hell, there were other documents in there." He massaged his temples. "He's into something massive."

"Get on with it," George barked.

"There's a schedule of when he receives drugs and who from—some geezer called Bakewell

Tart. Stupid fucking name if you ask me. The silly cunt even put the address of a lock-up on there. I went home, didn't know what to do, then went to the Lantern to speak to Precious, see if she knew anything about it."

"And did you?"

"No!" she said. "I only knew about the financial business and the brothel, fuck all about drugs."

George nodded to himself and eyed Boycie. "Go on."

"So I told her what I'd seen, and she said we had to tell you. I said all right, I've got nothing to hide, but we decided to go to the lock-up first this morning."

The drug delivery had been due, and if no one was there to receive it, Bakewell would have told Everett. They couldn't risk him suspecting something was up.

George smiled. "What did you find?"

"We had to break in for starters. It only had a padlock, so that was all right."

"And you just happened to have cutters on you?"

"Well yeah, I'm a tradesman. Carpenter."

And he was, so no lies there. Boycie had always worn gloves at the lock-up, a mask and sunglasses, so when taking in the gear, no one knew who he was. Thank God Roach had insisted on that, otherwise this wouldn't have worked.

"Fair enough." George gestured for him to continue.

"There was this filing cabinet in there, and in the drawers…" He hung his head then lifted it to stare at the wall between the twins' heads. "I still can't get over it. Packets of shit, like bricks. Weed in bags. Then Precious—she was outside, like—said someone was coming in a car. There was this box on the cabinet, had masks in it, like the ones from the pandemic, so we used them as well as the sunglasses we already had on. I didn't want us caught up in Everett's shit—I mean, I don't want to be looking over my shoulder for the rest of my natural if this Bakewell is a big player."

George waited patiently.

"So this bloke got out of a motor, black SUV, the flatbed sort. He came over and nodded. I didn't know what the fuck to do, and Presh was shitting herself, crying an' that. So I waited to see what happened. He loaded this big package onto a dolly, it had clingfilm wrapped all around it, was the size of a suitcase, and he pushed it inside the lock-up. He shook my hand and fucked off! We were crapping our pants, because I'd cut the fucking padlock and we couldn't secure the door, so in the end I just shut it and we came here. Asked the barmaid if she could get hold of you."

"Where's the lock-up?"

"Down Bold Street, unit seven."

George looked at Greg who got a phone out and tapped the screen.

"Shit, what are you doing?" Boycie said. "If Everett finds out what we've done…"

"Surveillance on the lock-up, Everett's house, his office, and checking out this Bakewell on the quiet for now," George said. "No need to panic, but we will be taking those drugs. Have you spoken to him today?"

Boycie shook his head. "No. I haven't even switched my phone on in case he's tried to get hold of me. I didn't trust myself not to ask him what the fuck he's playing at."

"What's the address of this Lantern place?"

Precious gave it. "Widow won't know what's going on if you barge in there, because she'll think everything's all right, you know, that Everett pays you for protection."

"Don't worry about that. Does he own the house?"

Boycie jumped in. "That's another thing I saw on the laptop. He pays the rent, but Widow's real name is on the lease. I thought that was a bit odd, considering he pays you protection. Why hide behind Widow?"

"But he doesn't pay us protection." George puffed air out. "Renting is an easy fix. We'll take the tenancy over, or offer to buy the house, and this Widow and the women there will then work for us. None of them need to know you grassed on their boss."

Shit, that means we'll be losing out on money. Boycie was meant to take over the brothel.

"Do you know where Everett is now?" George asked.

"I assume he'll be at the financial office," Precious said. "Or that's where I've always thought he worked. God, I hate him."

"When did you last see him?"

"Last night, before I went to work, before he went home and got smashed."

"As you work in the brothel, are you on the game?"

"No, I'm what he calls a greeter and flirter. I chat the punters up while they're waiting for a woman."

"Right. So what the fuck are you feeling now you know he's a liar?"

"I'm gutted. Not only because we've been mates for years, but I've been seeing him for months." She picked at skin beside a nail. "There's something else you should know."

"What…"

"I think he used to beat Alice up."

Boycie nodded. "Yeah, I've been thinking about that, remembering stuff from when I went round their gaff when they were married. She was a bit skittish, like she was scared, and he had a go at her a lot. Precious told me about videos. If she hit him, I reckon it was because she'd had enough. He says women should know their place, and I never liked the way he spoke to her, I said so to him a few times an' all, but he told me to mind my own business. The night before she was shot, we were round at Precious', she'd cooked us dinner, and he said something weird then, didn't he, Presh?"

She nodded. "He said he had a grudge against Alice but wouldn't say what it was."

George perked up. "Why didn't you tell us this when we came to your place yesterday?"

Precious let out a little wail. "Because he hits *me*. I'm shit-scared of him, which is why it took a lot of courage to come and see you two today. He's a nasty bastard if he doesn't get his own way, manipulative, a gaslighter, and I'm crapping myself in case he finds out it was us who grassed him up."

George laughed. "It's not like he can do anything to you now, though, is it? We'll go and collect him, and if he confesses, you'll never see him again."

Precious and Boycie had discussed Kayla and whether to drop *her* in the shit, too, and that weird Edna, but they'd gone against it. Kayla knew Precious was the shooter, so it was best to deal with her after everything had died down. As for Edna, Boycie said they could get her to take an overdose so it looked like she'd done it to herself. The problem with that was, it would happen after Roach had been rounded up. Would the twins believe he'd set that in motion already to happen later down the line? Would they even hear that Kayla and Edna had been offed?

Then there was Everett opening his mouth and telling them Precious and Boycie had known about everything all along. The only way to deal with that was to be there when the twins questioned him. With them thinking Everett was a gaslighter, they could swing it that he was doing the same to them.

"I want to be there when you talk to him," she said. "I want to hear the lies coming out of his mouth."

As planned, Boycie acted shocked. He whipped his head round to stare at her. "Fuck, no. What if he goes for you?"

George chuckled. "He'll be roped to a chair or strung up from the ceiling, so he won't be going for anyone."

"You're not facing him on your own," Boycie said. "I want to ask that cunt a few things an' all. He *lied* to us, Presh. For *years*. Jesus Christ."

George steepled his hands. "So let me get this straight. As far as you're aware, he's a financial consultant and a brothel owner. You thought we knew about the Lantern. You didn't know about the drugs and only suspect he hit Alice because of how he treats you, Precious. As soon as you discovered he's a drug dealer, you came to us. You ratted on your *friend*. Why?"

Boycie scoffed. "You think I want anything to do with *drugs*? Or going against you two? Fuck that. And mate or not, he's clearly been bullshitting us for a long time. I'm wondering now whether the financial consultant shit is all bollocks, a cover. He's got to be raking it in if he's shifting that much gear. It makes sense now why he only puts cash in the bank. None of his so-called clients pay by transfer or anything."

"What's that about?"

"Like I said, I sort his accounts before he sends them to a proper accountant. It's all cash."

"Sounds like he's strung you a big old line," George said. "Right, you two stay here. The woman on the desk, Amaryllis, she'll get you some food and drinks. Sit tight until we've picked Everett up. As you want to be there when we question him, we'll come back for you or send someone else. Fair warning, you'll be blindfolded. Our torture locations are a secret."

"Right." Boycie took Precious' hand. "It'll be all right."

She nodded and prayed that was true.

Chapter Twenty-Seven

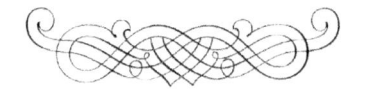

Ichabod Ahearn had been summoned to apprehend a man calling himself Bakewell Tart. He'd put a wig and beard on, plus fake glasses, gloves, and dark clothing he wouldn't mind burning. He never knew if blood would be involved until he was in the situation.

Cameron had found the fella after asking around, druggies eager to give up his real name for a few notes in their hands. Bakewell Tart, aka Rory Bakewell, lived in a bloody nice house. Cameron currently waited at the property, his car, courtesy of the twins' vehicle thief, Dwayne, parked behind an Audi out the front. Using binoculars, he'd spotted Bakewell inside at a dining table in the back of the living room, counting money. In a four-way message group, he'd given status updates so Ichabod knew the score before he arrived. The twins had remained silent on it, busy elsewhere.

Ichabod drew to a stop behind the nicked motor and got out, slipping into Cameron's passenger seat. "All right?"

"Yeah. He's switched from counting to packing gear into bricks. He's thick as pig shit, doing it in view of the window. He could at least have put nets up."

"Or a blind. Maybe he's so sure of himself he feels he'd never get caught. But packagin' in ye own house? Feckin' prick. Serves himself right that he's got found out."

"The patio doors are open round the back." Cameron jerked his head towards the house.

Ichabod took the binoculars and scoped the room out. And Bakewell. Medium-sized bloke, black hair, a bit of muscle on him. Nothing Ichabod couldn't take down with a few martial arts moves.

"He must feel secure," Ichabod said, "tae be doin' that in plain sight wid the doors open."

"I expect he doesn't know anyone's aware of where he lives. The scrotes who told me only know because they followed him one night. He'd been an arsehole to them, and while they were coked up to the eyeballs, they thought it'd be a good idea to do him over. But Bakewell had a few geezers here waiting for him, big blokes, so the druggies fucked off back to town."

Ichabod eyed the side of the house and a tall wooden gate that likely led to the rear garden. But with the windows so big, Bakewell would probably see them going down the front garden path.

"We'll have tae knock on the door. Or you will. I'll go round the back. Use ye initiative as tae why ye've paid him a visit."

"Right."

They got out, Ichabod following Cameron, hiding behind his massive size so if Bakewell glanced out, he'd only see one person. At the door, he darted to the left, tried the gate, but it was locked. He launched himself over just as Cameron knocked on the door. A quick zip down the alley, and he was on the patio, Bakewell gone from the table. Ichabod crept inside, glanced at the amount of drugs on a pallet on the floor, and shook his head. He moved towards the exit that led into the hallway.

"So can you do it?" Cameron asked. "It's just I was sent here by my boss who reckons you're the bloke we need."

Ichabod tiptoed up behind him.

"I'm fucking *livid* some fucker knows where I live. Who's this boss of yours?"

Cameron smiled. "Someone with a lot of clout."

Ichabod whipped his arm out and around, pressing it against Bakewell's throat at the same time bringing one of the twat's arms up behind his back. Bakewell struggled to get free, flapping his free arm, but with Ichabod applying more pressure to his Adam's apple, the munter sagged, going limp.

"Nice sleeper hold," Cameron said.

"Help me out, he's feckin' heavy."

Cameron stepped in and hefted Bakewell over his shoulder, turning to take him to the stolen car. Ichabod closed the door and, in the living room, closed the front curtains. He left via the patio, checking the door didn't have an auto lock. It didn't. Later, one of the twins' crews would probably come to collect the drugs and cash, payment for all the protection money Bakewell owed them.

He walked down the side of the house, gave the street the once-over, and nosed at what Cameron was up to. In the back seat, he'd cable tied Bakewell's wrists, gagged him, and the bloke was out of it, a bruise forming under one eye.

Ichabod got into his car, following Cameron out of the vicinity towards the prearranged meeting spot, where they'd wait for the twins to collect their cargo.

Chapter Twenty-Eight

Roach was getting sick of the bastard door being knocked on, not to mention angry as hell that neither Boycie nor Precious had got back to him. A worrying thought popped into his head that those two were fucking about between the sheets, Boycie making his move on her before Roach had given him permission. He'd be well narked if that's what was going on. Not that he cared about Precious enough to be hurt by her opening her legs to their mate, just that Boycie knew better than to do shit off his own bat.

He swung the door open, hoping either of them would be standing there, but it was the twins. His arsehole clenched at the sight of them. He hadn't expected to see them again, not now they'd watched the videos, so what the chuff did they want?

"All right, Everett?" George asked.

"Yes, not too bad, thank you."

"Not at work?"

"No, I took the day off. Alice and everything…"

"Yeah, must be upsetting, but look at it this way, your abuser is dead, so that's got to make you feel better, hasn't it?"

"That's a bit harsh, what with her mental health problems. She couldn't help what she did."

"Hmm. Anyway, we came to see how you are. We like our residents to feel safe in the knowledge that we have their backs."

Bloody hell, this was all he needed, those two popping in, being all buddy-buddy. "You don't need to worry about me. I'll be back at work tomorrow, trying to put this loss behind me."

He caught sight of someone walking towards them.

Oh, Jesus wept. What's she *doing coming over here?*

Max's wife rushed across the street, another glass dish in hand. It looked like either chilli or bolognese this time, condensation forming balls of liquid underneath the clingfilm lid.

"Sorry to butt in when you have visitors," she said, "but I've been batch cooking and thought you might like this. I don't dare give you any of the wellington, Max wouldn't be pleased. It's his favourite, and he usually has it for lunch the next day, too." She tittered and wedged herself between the twins.

"Kindly neighbour?" George asked her. "How lovely."

She stared up at him, then Greg. Paled. "Oh. Are you who I think you are?"

"Probably," George said. "And you are?"

"Isla. I live over the road."

"I see. And who's Max?"

"My husband." She thrust the dish at Roach then backed away. "I'd best get off…"

"Hold up." George turned to the side so he could see her. He smiled. "Did you know Alice?"

"Yes…"

"What did you make of her?"

"Oh, I wouldn't like to say, not now I know what she was *really* like."

"And what was that?"

"I can't tell you. It's not my story."

"It's okay," Roach said. "You can tell them."

"Well, she hit you, didn't she? I had no idea she was the type."

"People hide behind masks," George said, giving Roach a knowing look.

That gave him a jolt. Did they know who he was? That he wore a mask for the drug business? No, they couldn't. No one but Boycie and Precious knew he was Roach. Paranoia was a bitch, and he shook it off.

Isla nodded. "I really should get home. Max is finishing early today, and we're going out for dinner."

"What, you're not going to eat any of that batch cooking?" George asked.

"We always go out after I've made the week's food. I never want to eat something I've cooked if I've slaved over it all day." It seemed like she wanted to tell them it was none of their business but stopped herself.

"That wellington pastry will go all soggy if you don't eat it today."

"It'll be fine. Can I...can I go home now?"

"No one's stopping you," George said.

But you did. You asked her questions.

Roach admired the way the bloke fucked with people's heads. George had just gaslit her, and Isla didn't appear to have a clue. It reminded Roach of Alice, how she hadn't twigged for ages what he was up to, and by the time he'd recorded those videos, she'd been on the verge of believing she was having 'episodes' and she beat up her husband.

If only she hadn't told her friends...

They'd probably still be married now, Alice a total wreck, so compliant he had total control over her. But it had all gone wrong. Still, there was always the next one, and he might well teach those friends a lesson one day.

Isla scuttled off, George watching her until she'd closed her front door.

"Nice woman," he said as he turned back to Roach.

"She fed me when Alice first left, as did a few others. They felt sorry for me, banded together to make sure I was okay."

"Did any of them know her well?"

"No, she kept to herself. I tried to get her to go out on a date with me, Isla, and Max, but she wasn't having any of it." He ignored the fact Alice and Isla used to talk in the street sometimes. He'd often wondered whether his ex-wife had spilled the beans about him, but Isla had never looked at him funny. He must have scared Alice so much she'd kept her gob shut. Until she'd met those friends. Which reminded him, he had to find out if the twins had been nosing into things like the police were. "I need to let her mates know she's died, but I don't even know who they are. She never did mention their names."

"She told us about them when she moved into the refuge," George said.

"How do you know?"

George smiled. "It's *our* refuge."

Roach acted shocked. "*What*? You knew Alice before all this kicked off? Before she was shot?"

"Yeah."

"You never said."

"We don't have to." George smiled again. "Anyway, fancy a bevvy down the Noodle?"

"I'm not really in the mood."

"What *are* you in the mood for? We can smoke weed, or there's always cocaine. We're not fussy."

George didn't look odd, and he didn't sound odd, but Roach's intuition flared to life. Or was it because he was a major dealer and the words 'weed' and 'coke' had tripped his suspicion switch?

"I'm not into drugs, mate, but thanks for the offer. I appreciate it. Anyway, I'd best get going."

"Off somewhere, are you?"

"No, but the washing doesn't do itself."

"Taking advantage of the nice weather?"

"Something like that." *Why won't they just fuck off?*

"Take a break. Come on, a pint or two will do you good," George insisted. "I might get offended if you don't take me up on the offer."

The warning had been stated as a joke, but was it fuck.

"All right, but not for long. I didn't sleep much last night and need a kip." He'd slept like the dead, but he wasn't lying, he could do with a nap.

He'd been wondering if the coke he'd had was from a dodgy batch, the way it had got to him so quickly, and he hadn't felt right after sniffing it at all. He'd have to get hold of Bakewell, warn him in case other people almost overdosed on the stuff.

He collected his keys from the dish on the side table and followed George to a black cab. Kayla had mentioned they drove one sometimes, as well as a battered white van and their infamous BMW. He got in the back, George climbing in with him. Anxious about the man sitting so close, Roach pretended he wasn't bothered, but he was. The air seemed to bristle with menace.

"Actually, I really should get some kip," he said, moving to open the door.

George slapped a hand on Roach's thigh and whipped a gun out, holding it low and pointing it at his stomach. "Now then, I've been polite so far, but you're getting right on my fucking tits, son. So sit there nicely and shut up while my brother takes us for a little drive."

Roach eyed the gun. "What…what's going on?"

"You'll soon find out. We're off to see Bakewell Tart."

Oh God. Fuck. Shit! Calm down, he never saw your face. "A cake? What?"

"Don't play innocent, sunshine."

Roach glanced out of the window. Despite him shutting the front door, it now stood open. Greg came out, carrying his laptop. He slammed the door and strode towards the taxi, getting in and putting the laptop on the passenger seat. He drove away as if a gun wasn't in the picture and there was nothing to worry about.

"I don't understand," Roach said, although he understood perfectly well. Some cunt had grassed him up.

Greg stared at him in the rearview. "You will."

Chapter Twenty-Nine

George had a feeling Roach would opt for his gaslighting ways and try to convince everyone *they* were in the wrong and not him. Call it survival instinct or desperation, but he'd bet fifty quid the tosser thought he'd covered his arse in all aspects. The financial consultant job was a front just as much as Jackpot Palace and the

Noodle were theirs, except he'd fucked up by his supposedly cash-only payments.

The fact he clouted Precious was another black mark against him. Alice must have been telling the truth, and now George had had time to think back to those videos, rather than her coming off as an outright drunken nutter, he saw her as a woman trying hard to stick up for herself against a man who'd told her she suffered from 'episodes'.

As for the brothel, not a problem, the women's jobs were still safe, but the drugs were another matter. Later, a crew would go in and collect the gear from Bakewell's house once it got dark, and another had already picked up the large stash at Everett's lock-up. George had wanted the gear as quickly as possible in case the police poked into Everett some more and discovered he rented a hideaway. Moon had agreed to take the drugs off their hands to keep them and suspicion off Cardigan, and they'd split the profits later down the line.

Everett had been a good boy, keeping quiet on the journey, but George doubted it would be long before he opened his trap, especially when he saw Bakewell Tart. Greg pulled up behind a disused petrol station and parked between Ichabod's and Cameron's cars.

"What's happening?" Everett said.

"Shut your mush." Greg turned round, his own gun aimed at Everett. "You sit nice and tight while my brother goes and gets Bakewell."

George put his gun away and took a cable tie out of his pocket. He secured Everett's wrists, despite the bloke creating a fuss by trying to hide his hands. "I wouldn't advise that you fuck me about, my old son. You're getting right on my last nerve, and that's never a good thing." He got out and approached Cameron's car, peering in the back at a black-haired bloke who'd been gagged and bound. He glanced up at Ichabod who'd got out of his car. "All right, mate?"

"Yeah. I knocked the eejit out wid a sleeper hold, but he came round about ten minutes ago. Cameron carried him tae the car, so there might be a problem if someone saw it. As far as I could tell, it's the type of street where everyone's out at work, but ye can never be too sure."

"Right, well, I'm not bothered. You're both in disguise and the motors are nicked. Leave yours here so Dwayne can sell it on, it's too good to burn it out or crush it." George opened the back door of Cameron's car and dragged Bakewell out. He propped him on his feet, holding him up by the scruff of the neck. "Nice and awake now, are we?"

Bakewell said something, but the gag muffled it.

"Don't know what you're on about, mate." George nodded to Ichabod. "We'll give you a lift back on the way."

Ichabod walked off and got in the front of the taxi.

Cameron emerged from the car. "There's a pallet of gear in his living room and cash in a safe on the sideboard in there."

"Cheers. Go and drop the car with the crusher then go home to Janine."

Cameron nodded and drove the old Ford away. Bakewell said something else, sounding frantic, but George wasn't interested in garbled bullshit.

"You can tell me all about it once we get to where we're going." He guided him to the taxi, shoving him inside next to Everett. "Any funny business, and I'll shoot." He went to the boot, taking out two blindfolds. He'd got a bargain box of sleep masks off Amazon, which was handy, because the dead kid's dad might want in on this, and he'd need his eyes covered on the way there.

George poked his head in the back of the taxi and slid a blindfold on Bakewell, jogging to the other side to do the same to Everett. Both men's hands were tied in front of them, so they could easily move the fabric, but he'd give them a little warning that they really shouldn't.

He got in beside Bakewell, smiling at Ichabod in the passenger seat. "Move those blindfolds, and I'll shoot you in the bollocks, got it?"

Everett dipped his head, but Bakewell whimpered.

"Off you go then, Greg. We'll pop Ichabod to the casino then nip round and see Kenny Feldon."

The taxi peeled away, and George took his gun out and pressed it to the side of Bakewell's head for fun. "Are you shitting yourself, son? Because you should be."

Chapter Thirty

Edna had the urge to run. Not from her life or what she'd done, but actually run. A manic phase had descended, and her limbs twitched, her need to get moving taking over. She quickly put on her jogging gear and did some warm-ups, stretching out her legs that had knots in the calves. A minute or so later she left the bungalow, her red baseball cap pulled low. She started at a steady pace, even though her body screamed for her to sprint. A right at the end of the street, and she went down Grover Road, the long one that led to the corner shop and the chippy at the end. A black cab sailed by, and she automatically tensed, her steps faltering. It stopped outside one of the houses, and…shit, George got out.

Edna kept going. If she stopped now and went back the other way, he'd clock her, she was too close for him not to. However, he didn't take any notice, unless he watched her from the corner of his eye, and strode up a garden path. She continued on, glancing in at back seat of the taxi, catching a glimpse of two men, both with blindfolds on. Greg sat in the driver's seat, so she ducked her head, then realised he could have been watching her in the wing mirror.

Fucking hell!

She jogged on, dying to look back and see what was going on. Who was George visiting? She dipped down an alley between houses and stopped out of sight beside one of four wheelie bins. Taking her cap off, she poked half her face round the corner of the house and watched. George spoke to someone, but she couldn't see who it was. Then he turned and got in the back of the taxi. A man left the house and sat in the passenger seat, then the taxi headed off.

Edna dashed to crouch behind a bin farther along so no one would see her. She peeped out, the taxi sailing by, Greg staring down the alley. Shit, he'd seen her as she'd gone past him. He'd watched where she'd gone. Had he recognised her? Would they pay her another visit?

The sound of the engine changed, so she thought they'd turned down a side street off Grover Road. She slapped her cap back on and ran out of the alley, planning to continue her run.

But the taxi had reversed to a few metres along and idled at the kerb.

Should she keep running or stop to talk to them? Go home?

The decision was made for her. Greg got out and stepped onto the pavement, blocking her way. She had no choice but to stop.

"How's it going, Edna? I'm glad we saw you as we wanted a word."

Shit. What was going on? Her mind threw up a frightening scenario. Had Roach told them she'd worked at Haven and given her that ridiculous disguise? Someone had come and collected it from her back garden, but had he given it to them so they could get someone to do a DNA test on it and prove she'd been a mole?

"I've told you," she said, "I don't know who this other Edna is."

"Don't panic. We just wanted you to know that it's been confirmed someone borrowed your name. Do you know a man called Everett?"

"Nope."

"Are you sure? Because if we find out you do…"

"I don't know anyone who goes by that name."

"I saw you nosing in the back of the cab. What did you see?"

"Two men in blindfolds."

"Wrong answer. You saw nothing."

"Right. I saw nothing."

He smiled. "Enjoy your run."

He moved out of her path, and she picked up her pace, keeping it steady so he didn't think he'd frightened her. But her brain ticked over too fast, and her body itched again where it wanted her to run and run and run until she was sick. The taxi went past her, Greg holding up a hand in a wave. He scowled when she didn't return the gesture.

She jogged on, wondering if she may live to regret that.

Chapter Thirty-One

Kayla hadn't deleted Edna's number like she'd been told to. You never knew when contacts would come in handy, did you? Her phone, still ringing from when she'd left work a minute ago, had Kayla curious as to what Edna wanted. She nipped down the side of the building and swiped the screen.

"Hello?"

"It's me."

"I know, your name was on my phone. What's the matter?"

"I think I saw Roach in the back of the twins' taxi. He had a blindfold on, but I recognised the hair at his temple, the way it curls funny. There was another man with a blindfold as well."

"Why are you even telling me this?"

"Because of what we did for him at Haven. If he's with the twins… We could be right in the shit if he opens his mouth."

"Don't be daft. He'd never tell on us."

Kayla had sounded blasé, but she was shitting herself. Had George and Greg found out what Everett had organised, or had they picked him up thinking he'd killed Alice? And who the hell was the other blindfolded bloke?

"Greg saw me. He spoke to me," Edna said.

"What did he say?"

"He thinks someone used my name."

"Then that means they don't know you were at Haven." But what if they'd finally found out Vicky Hart was some random cow in Essex? What if they came back to question Kayla? "Look, don't worry about it. No one can prove you were there. You had a body suit and mask on, for fuck's sake."

"Okay."

"Just get on with your life and stick to the story."

"What if Roach tells them about me?"

"Then you deny it. Now calm down. Go and make a cuppa or something." Kayla cut the call and walked out onto the street towards the bus stop. She boarded the bus, pushing her worries aside. Until she sat and thought about it. If George and Greg had Everett, that could mean the end of his business. She wouldn't get to work at the brothel or do other jobs for him.

At the end of her journey, she got off and rushed up to Precious' flat, knocking on the door. No one answered, so she walked along the balcony and let herself into her own place. Cooper lay on the sofa, and she lifted his feet so she could sit down, placing them on her lap. She told him about Edna's call.

"So you're going to have to be careful," she said. "If they're poking into Everett's business, that means they might put a watch on the flats again to keep an eye on Precious."

"I still worked when their blokes were watching before, so stop panicking."

How could she stop, though? It wasn't Cooper who'd end up with a Cheshire. They had no idea he was Parker, and she wasn't about to grass him up.

But could she say the same for him? The answer was she didn't know, and that brought her up short. Yes, he was the right man for her, they got along well, but if it came to saving his own skin, would he feed her to the wolves?

Chapter Thirty-Two

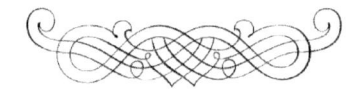

Precious and Boycie had been careful not to say anything incriminating in the room at The Angel when they'd been on their own. Fuck knows if the twins had hidden CCTV somewhere. After a sandwich and a hot chocolate, caged in and feeling it, Precious had asked Amaryllis if she thought the twins would mind them waiting out the back. The woman had said it was likely okay, so they'd gone outside.

"How do you think it went?" Precious whispered.

"I think we've done the easy part," Boycie whispered back.

"What do you mean? I was crapping myself in there. That was hard!"

"But it'll be even harder to convince them once Roach starts spouting about us being involved from the start. He'll say you killed Alice, he'll want to save himself, and then what? If George and Greg don't believe us, we're fucked."

"We've been through this. We know exactly what to say."

Boycie sighed. "Yeah, well, I'm just getting jittery, that's all."

"We can't let him get away with treating us like shit, and if we want to be together…" Cruel of her, but it had to be said to remind him of what his goal was. "We'll get through it. Two of us against him, both acting like whatever he'll say is news to us. I can cry convincingly, you know that."

He leaned against the wall and stared towards the graveyard. "I still give a shit about him, that's the problem."

"I know, because you thought he was someone else, that's all. That other shit on the laptop you didn't tell the twins about must have really upset you."

"I didn't know he thought I was a lapdog, a prick. I didn't know he imagined killing me."

"Who writes rap songs on a laptop his friend uses to update his accounts? Honestly. You could have seen that way before now. And as for him thinking he's a rapper…"

He laughed sadly. "He's a bit of a knob, really, isn't he."

"Yep."

"He wrote stuff about you, too."

For some reason, that didn't hurt her. She'd guessed as much. "Go on then, what did he say about me?"

"It was sexual. Kinky stuff."

"Gross."

She felt for Boycie, especially as the twins might get to see the raps about him. Roach had been an utter wanker with the things he'd said. Popping Boycie if he got on his nerves too much, burying him in the woods. Or maiming him, cutting his tongue out so he couldn't speak. So many scenarios had been worked into song stories, most of them involving Boycie, all with the theme that he was a stupid little lackey who'd be nothing without Roach. Thank fuck they didn't have anything in them about Boycie dealing with drugs, but there might be others in files he hadn't had time to check.

Precious had to remind him of how disloyal Roach had been. "Why? Why pick on his best friend? You've been like a brother to him for bloody years. Just for that alone we're doing the right thing. Then there's Alice and what she went through."

"Bastard."

She stood in front of him and leaned in for a cuddle, her cheek on his chest. "It'll be all right. We'll get him killed, then we can move on."

"Knowing our luck, the police will think I've done it because I'll inherit his house and money."

Her head shot up. "Shit, we're going to have to ask the twins if they can dump his body somewhere. No body, no money."

He rested his forehead on hers. "Fuck's sake, I didn't think of that. Then there's the fact it'll be suss that Alice was killed, then him."

"The coppers will likely look at both of us, but we're each other's alibi. We spent the whole day and evening in my flat, right?"

He nodded.

An engine rumbled, and she broke away from him to peer round the side of the pub. The taxi pulled into the side car park, and Greg spotted her, beckoning her forward.

She turned to Boycie. "It's time to go."

Chapter Thirty-Three

Colin hadn't thought he'd sleep after finding his wife dead, but he'd been so exhausted since making a statement at the station, he'd handed over his clothes, per procedure, borrowed a tracksuit used for prisoners, found a Premier Inn because his house was now a crime scene, and fallen into bed. He'd spent the day with Janine, although Sheila Sutton had told him he could go back home about seven tonight. Janine had been brilliant, and she'd talked him out of doing away with himself.

That had been the overriding urge for most of the morning, to take tablets with booze and end it all. To go wherever the missus had gone. They were supposed to be with each other way into their eighties. The end wasn't meant to be now.

He had an awful fire in his belly, the flames made of retribution, anger, and the need to find whoever the fuck had killed her and slice his throat. It was so unfair, for it to end like this. A cruel jibe at what he did for a living—you want to learn to have more empathy for the families of victims? Here, experience it yourself so you *really* know how to dish out platitudes. And it was true, what some people had said to him in his time as a police officer: "You'll never know what I'm going through unless you go through it yourself."

Never could he have imagined the gnawing hatred, the utter devastation losing her had brought. And the selfish thoughts that had come unbidden, which he hated himself for: Was the life insurance up to date? Was that bastard going to come for him next?

"Talk to me, Col," Janine said.

He glanced across at her from his seat on her sofa. "For the first time in my life, I think I have it in me to kill someone."

"It's a bit of a revelation when that happens, isn't it?"

"Yeah. I never put me down as someone who'd do that, but I've been imagining it. All the blood, the satisfaction, but it won't bring her back, will it, so what's the point?"

"You'll feel better. You'll have done something for her, to get justice. The twins will look into this whether you like it or not. They'll try to find him, and when they do, they'll ask if you want to be there to kill him."

"Not if the police find him first."

"A bit hard when he used a condom. There's fuck all to identify him. No DNA anywhere on her."

Nigel had been round to deliver that news. Of course *he* was on the bloody case, but Colin wasn't allowed to partner him. Understandable, and anyway, he'd decided to take a month off, but fucking hell, having Nigel poking into his life, knowing all the ins and outs... And would he even *find* the bastard?

"Tell them I'll be there," Colin said.

"What?"

"Actually, tell them I'm interested in the job." He'd been thinking of it periodically ever since he'd stood out the front waiting for his colleagues to arrive last night. If he couldn't get justice for his wife, he'd fucking well get it some other way, for other people.

"Are you sure?"

"Yes. No. But do it anyway." He sat back and closed his eyes.

Chapter Thirty-Four

Roach's armpits screamed in pain. He didn't know where he was—the blindfold was still on, and someone had stuffed a rag in his mouth—but he'd been stripped and strung up somewhere. This wasn't how he'd envisage his life ending, and he didn't intend for it to happen this way. He'd do and say whatever it took to get out of this.

His mind spun with possibilities. Who'd grassed him up? Bakewell? Or, and he didn't want to entertain this but had to, was it Precious or Boycie? Neither of them had checked in today, and that wasn't normal.

A cold sluice of dread went through him as he recalled last night. Working on the spreadsheet, sniffing a few lines while he was at it. Boycie turning up. Putting him to bed. Had he looked at the laptop after? Roach couldn't remember if he'd shut it or not, but it had been closed this morning.

Christ. All those raps he'd written on the nights Boycie had naffed him off. He hadn't *meant* it. He didn't want the bloke dead, it had just been a way to get his angst out. What if Boycie had seen them? Got angry and dobbed him in? No, he wouldn't be that stupid. Roach could get him in the shit for all sorts. Then again, with his rule of covering their faces and using code names via texts, *could* he?

Fuck it. In ensuring his own anonymity, he'd also ensured Boycie's.

What about Precious, then? She'd been weird with him yesterday. Could Boycie have told her what he'd seen and *she'd* taken the reins? Talked him into telling The Brothers?

The eerie quiet unsettled him.

Had the twins strung Bakewell up, too? No one had spoken after they'd stopped somewhere to pick someone up. Who was it? The person who'd engineered it so he currently hung from the fucking ceiling?

Apart from Precious and Boycie, the only other person who knew he dealt with Bakewell was Edna. He'd bragged to her once about being in with one of the big dealers, stupidly mentioning his name.

What the fuck did you think you were doing?

He'd become what his father had predicted, a big-headed twat who didn't know when to keep his mouth shut.

And now the chickens were coming home to roost.

Chapter Thirty-Five

George started with Bakewell. After all, the bloke had already pissed himself, so it seemed he was the easiest one to crack. The cottage didn't have enough hooks in the ceiling to hang them both up, so after stripping him, he'd pushed Mr Tart over to the corner to the left of the door. A puddle of urine lay beneath him on the steel floor, seeping into the material of his gag discarded nearby. The smell wasn't too pleasant, so George got hold of the mop and bucket and cleaned it up, kicking Bakewell's outer thigh to signal he needed to move across out of the way.

With everyone but the two naked men in forensic outfits, the door to the steel room locked so Precious, Boycie, and Kenny Feldon could take their blindfolds off, the scene was set. Precious and Boycie stood against the wall, Everett in front of them, and Kenny sat beside them on a fold-out chair. Greg had pulled another chair over and currently sat near the door.

"Did you ever make one of your customers piddle their pants?" George asked Bakewell. "It's just…I'm wondering if now the shoe's on the other foot, whether you wish you'd been a nicer person."

The man let out a sob, snot falling onto his top lip. Tears dribbled from beneath the blindfold.

"Would you like to see what's going on?" George asked. "Where you are an' all that?"

"No…"

"Hmm, I wouldn't either. Who do you get your gear off? You're clearly a middle man. Who's the top dog in the chain?"

"I can't tell you."

"See, this is what I don't get. Unless your family's been threatened, of *course* you can tell me—they're not going to kill you when they find out you've blabbed because you'll already be dead."

"W-what?"

"Fuck me, what did you think this was, a little chat, then you can go on your merry way? Not a chance. You're not leaving here alive. Who do you buy from?"

"I don't know his real name, but he goes by Crisp, and the one above him is Biscuit."

"Fucking hell, it's right old picnic, what with you being a tart. Are you all named after food?"

"Probably."

"Who do you sell to?"

"Three different blokes."

"And what are their names?"

"Nomad, Roach, and Custard."

"Only one of them is food. What does that mean?"

"Fuck knows, I just know them as that."

"Where are they based?"

Bakewell reeled off three lock-up addresses, two of them on Cardigan, the other on the Moon

Estate. George turned to Greg who nodded and got their phone out. Surveillance would be sent out to the other Cardigan lock-up, as Everett's had already been dealt with, and he expected Moon would deal with the one on his turf.

"When were their last drop-offs?"

"This morning."

"So they're not due more until next week?"

"That's right, unless they run out, then I have to give them more. Can I...can I go home now? I swear I won't do this again."

"No, you won't..."

"Fuck..."

"Yeah, sorry, mate, but you've been supplying without permission, and I expect you know the rules."

"But Biscuit said you knew."

George smiled. "I expect he told you to say that if you ever got caught, too. What type of biscuit is he?"

"What?"

"Come on, I'd like to know. Custard Cream? Hobnob? Rich Tea?"

"I don't *know*! They're just a name to me, I don't see faces."

"Do you cover yours?"

"No."

"Bit stupid."

"Jesus Christ, please, I—"

"Don't waste your breath. How long have you been selling to Roach?"

"Years. He started off small, then his business grew."

George stooped down to remove Bakewell's blindfold. He walked over to the hanging Everett and twisted him round so Pissy Boy could see him. "Recognise him or anyone else in this room?"

Bakewell blinked in the harsh light. Glanced around at Precious, Boycie, Kenny, Greg, then Everett. "N-no, only you and your brother."

"Right." George looked over at Precious and Boycie. "Recognise him?"

Boycie nodded. "He's the man at the lock-up this morning."

Everett grunted—oh, had he only just realised his mate had grassed him up?

Wait until you hear Precious' voice…

George smiled at her. "What about you, love?"

She nodded, too. "Yes, that's him."

Everett screamed through gritted teeth.

"Shut your face, you." George poked him in the side. "Your turn will come to have your say." He returned to Bakewell, grabbing his upper arm and hauling him to his feet. He manoeuvred him to stand against the wall. "Now then, I don't usually do this, but I'm going to let you choose the way you die—so long as it's quick. Not being rude, but I want you done and dusted because Mad really wants to get going on Everett."

"I don't know any Everett."

"Roach, then. So what way do you want to go out?"

Bakewell's cock dribbled piss again. "Oh God, fucking hell… Just shoot me in the head, for Pete's sake."

George pulled down the zip of his forensic suit and took his gun out. He zipped up again then pressed the business end of the weapon to the bloke's brow. Watched the fear flickering in his eyes, all those last, frantic thoughts, maybe his life flashing before him—fun times, regrets, all that shit.

"You should have thought of that before you went into the drugs game, son." George stepped back a metre or so and pulled the trigger.

Bakewell's arms flew up, his torso jolting, then he slid to the floor, the back of his head seeming attached to the wall. A wide smear of blood dirtied the steel, along with brain matter and fuck knew what else, and he came to rest in a sitting position, his chin touching his chest. Blood meandered around the sides of his neck to form mini rivers down his pecs. George moved forward to inspect the back of the ruined head; the brain had a big chunk missing. Nice.

He sniffed. "Well, that's him sorted. Now for you, Everett."

George spun round and stalked to stand in front of him. He reached up and drew the blindfold off, tossing it to the floor. Ripped the fabric out of his mouth and dropped it. He swivelled him round on the chain so he could see Bakewell. "That bloke there got off lightly. Normally, I like to string things out and *really* hurt people. I've pulled off finger and toenails, chopped fingers and toes off—noses even. Ears. Tongues. I've stretched people, crushed them, sliced their dicks off. I've done so many nasty things I can't even remember them all. But unlike our Mr Tart, you're not going to have the choice of how you die. See, we now know you had Alice killed, and because of you, this man here lost his son."

George gestured to Kenny who, now it had come right down to it, didn't seem as eager to end a life as he had before.

"So, why don't you do this man a courtesy and tell him exactly why his lad was murdered by whoever you picked to do the job. I'm sure he'd like to know whether his son died in vain."

Everett flicked his eyes in his friends' direction. He stared at Boycie for ages, shook his head sadly, then gave Precious a filthy look. "She killed Alice, and he knew all about it from start to finish."

"What?" Precious screeched. "You're such an arsehole. Why the fuck would *I* kill her?"

"You offered," Everett said. "I was all for getting someone else to do it, but you stepped up and said *you'd* do it." He shook his head and faced George. "You'll find all the gear she wore in the lock-up. Motorbike leathers, the lot."

"It's already been searched. Nothing of the kind in there." George paced, giving himself a moment to dissect Everett's accusation and Precious' reaction to it. She'd looked appalled yet at the same time as if she'd known he'd try to turn it around on her. "Precious was shopping. We have her on CCTV."

"Not for the exact time of the shooting," Everett said. "She'd have appeared in town half an hour later."

True. Bennett had confirmed Precious had been in town but her exact time of entering the long street wasn't recorded. He'd first seen her coming out of Costa but not going in. Not unusual, he'd said, as he and his colleague moved the cameras to scan potential suspects, shoplifters and the like. She'd likely entered town at a point when they'd been distracted or from the rear of Costa where they had a patio with chairs and tables easily accessible from the street behind. No CCTV at that point, though—or not a working camera anyway. She could have been in Costa when the shooting took place.

George turned to her. "Where exactly were you in town when you first got there?"

"Costa," she said.

"Got a receipt or proof that you bought something in there?"

"I used cash, and no, I don't have a receipt. Someone will have seen me in there, though, surely."

George nodded. He'd said this for Everett's benefit. Making out he didn't trust Precious, when they'd already had their alibis checked. Someone *had* seen her in Costa. They'd sat at the table next to her. Someone had already looked into what Boycie had been doing. He'd fixed broken bed slats at some old dear's house. Her video doorbell had captured him going in and out. And then there was Everett, undeniably in the Noodle. If it wasn't any of those three, who the fuck was it?

He smiled at the bloke. "Look, I'll come clean. I'm just fucking about. I know your mates didn't do anything, and neither did you, but I'd like to know who it was so we can get them picked up."

"I'm telling you, it was *her*."

Precious stepped forward. "I can't believe you'd blame it on me to get yourself out of the shit. Don't I mean anything to you?"

"Not really, no. You were always the third wheel."

Precious swiped tears from her face. "I should have known you were using me for sex. You only ever want me when there's no one else around. As for you dealing drugs… What the hell? How the fuck did you keep that from us all this time?"

"You've known all along, you lying little skank."

She looked at George. "He's bullshitting. There's no way I'd have anything to do with him if he was dealing." She shifted her gaze to Everett. "Was that where you went on the nights neither of us could get hold of you? Were you distributing your gear?"

"You know damn well what I was doing." Everett glared at Boycie. "Especially you, because you were with me."

Boycie held his hands up, palms facing Everett. "I don't know what you're on about, mate, but if you're thinking of dragging me into your mess, then think again. The first I heard you dealt drugs was last night when I saw shit on your laptop."

Everett closed his eyes and laughed wryly. "You're a clever cunt, I'll give you that much. What did she do, blab that you're inheriting everything? Yeah, it all makes fucking sense now."

"What's he on about?" George asked.

Boycie shrugged. "No idea."

Everett opened his eyes and appealed to Precious. "Come on, admit I told you Boycie would be left everything."

"When?" she said, frowning.

"You know when. You asked me about the business and what would happen to it if I died."

"I have no idea what you're on about," she said. "You're just making shit up now."

He laughed, head thrown back. Then screamed, staring at the ceiling, eyes bulging. Kenny seemed taken aback, clearly unused to such a display of anger. He nervously glanced at Precious who shrugged as if this was normal.

"He gets like this when he's been caught out," she said above the din.

Everett stopped. Glared at her. "You are a slut of the highest fucking order. Happy with yourself, are you? Setting me the fuck up with *my* best mate? What did you do, promise him use of your sloppy-seconds cunt?"

Precious rushed forward and punched him in the dick. He brought his knees up, trying to protect the area, but she punched him again. He groaned, eyes shut and watering, then laughed, bordering on mania.

Boycie shook his head. "Happens every fucking time. He'll be needing coke. He always goes manic like this when he's due a sniff."

Everett shut up and stared at him. "All we've been through, and it came to this."

"I don't like drugs, mate, you know that. And when I found out what you were doing behind our backs, I had to dob you in. Sorry, but you know how I feel about being on the straight and narrow. I'd never have gone to see Widow with condoms and whatever if I'd known the brothel wasn't legit either. Who the fuck do you think you are, making out me and Presh are in on this? I thought we meant more to you than that, but then again, you've always been a selfish bastard, only out for yourself. And as for Alice…why couldn't you have just left her alone?"

Everett's eyes widened, the look of a nutter taking over his features. "Because she wasn't allowed to get away with it like my Mum did!"

Silence as everyone stared at him. Was this it, the real reason he'd had a woman killed? George was well aware that childhood could fuck you up, get its claws into you until you couldn't see straight, but…

"What did your mum do?" George asked.

"She brought up a monster, that's what she did," Kenny shouted and ran at him, an axe raised level with his head.

He brought it down, right in the centre of Everett's chest, the thick blade embedded. Everett's body rocked, pushing Kenny backwards so he let go of the handle and stumbled to bump into the wall beside Precious. Blood seeped around the blade, dribbling from the corners of Everett's mouth. He smiled, laughing, his teeth stained red, then he roared, fists clenched, the pain kicking in. George glanced at Kenny to see if he wanted to continue, but Precious hugged the poor bloke, his face turned away.

George raised his eyebrows at Boycie. "Do you want to finish him off?"

Boycie shook his head.

George sighed and walked over to his tool table. Picked up a machete. On his way back to Everett, he thought about Alice, how kind and gentle she'd been, and how—although he felt guilty about it now—he'd almost thought *she'd* been the deranged one. He slashed the blade through the air, slicing off a chunk of Everett's upper arm, and he kept slashing. Blood sheeted over his form to drip from his feet. George had left the face intact, wanting Kenny to see, right until the end, exactly who'd caused his son to die. He paused, out of breath, to check if the bloke was dead yet. No. He rasped an exhale, hanging on by one arm as George had hacked through the other at the elbow, apparently. He'd been unaware, Mad taking over.

He placed the machete back on the table and gripped Everett's ankles, pulling his legs to one side. "Greg, open that trapdoor, will you?"

"Wait!" Precious said. "What happens now? What will you do with the body?"

"He'll rot under this building. Why?"

"What about the brothel and everything? He said he left it to Boycie…"

"It doesn't matter," Boycie said. "It's tainted money anyway."

George eyed him. The bloke seemed genuine. "She's right. If he's left shit to you, then you should have it." He glanced at the partial arm still hanging from a manacle. "I'll drop that arm and his head off somewhere. The rest of him can go under there."

He picked a sword up and stood to the side of Everett, lining it up as if about to hit a golf ball.

He swung, the blade eating into the throat and coming out on the other side. The head thudded to the floor, and George kicked it away. It came to rest in Bakewell's last dribble of piss.

George smiled. "I reckon that's a job well done, don't you?"

"I need to get out of here," Kenny said. "I'm going to be sick…"

Funny how the sight and smell of blood got to people like that.

Chapter Thirty-Six

Precious woke to the sound of knocking on the flat door. She sat up, patting Boycie lying next to her. "Wake up. Someone's here." The knocking continued, and she'd bet it'd be the coppers. "Fuck's sake, wake up!"

Boycie jolted upright then bounded out of bed. She grabbed her dressing gown off the hook on the wall and left the room. She'd lived alone for so long she hadn't even considered whether Boycie would want to go down first—and Everett hadn't been the type to put himself in the firing line if someone else was there to do it for him.

She stalked to the front door, snapping on the outside light. Two shapes stood behind the glass—she recognised one of them. Nigel bloody Hampton. She opened up, sensing Boycie right behind her.

"What time d'you call this?" she asked, squinting at them.

The woman with Nigel checked her watch. "Two thirty-three a.m." She smiled. "DC Bach, by the way."

"And?" Boycie came to stand next to Precious. "What's going on?"

Nigel glanced left and right along the balcony. "Can we come in?"

"Of course, but what's happened?" Precious stepped back and wandered into the living room on purpose. They'd left messy bedding on the sofa for exactly this moment, and if the police had come during the day, that bedding would be folded neatly on the armchair.

She sat on the sofa where it looked like Boycie had flung the quilt back when the pigs had knocked on the door. The only issue would be that it wasn't warm, and Precious wouldn't put it past Nigel to check. She'd discussed every single aspect with Boycie, and he'd remembered what she'd said—he sat at the pillow end of the sofa, drawing the quilt over him to cover his boxer shorts.

Bach stayed in the doorway.

Nigel stood by the armchair, then lowered onto it. "When was the last time you saw Everett?"

Precious frowned. "Um, let me think. The day Alice died. Or the evening, I should say. He was here for dinner, then left when I went to work. He rang me a few times this morning, but I was asleep—I work into the early hours, although it's my night off now. Why?"

"What about you?" Nigel asked Boycie.

"The same night. I went round his house and put him to bed."

"Put him to bed?"

"Um, yeah, he's got a habit of doing too much of the white stuff lately, if you know what I mean. He rang me to go over there. Think he was panicking he'd OD'd? Anyway, by the time I got there, he was half asleep, so I carried him upstairs."

"What time was this?"

"I can't really remember. Hang on..." He checked his call log and told them when Everett had rung. "Then there's missed calls this morning, because I was asleep an' all."

"Where was this?"

Boycie gestured to the settee. "Here. It's my bed sometimes. I kip here when I can't be arsed to go home. We were chatting about how bad his drug use has got."

Nigel nodded. "Right. Um, we've just come from his father's house where body parts were discovered... Sorry to have to tell you, but Everett has been murdered."

Precious shot to her feet. "What?"

"Fuck me," Boycie said, staring at the floor. "First Alice, now him? Are they linked?"

"They may well be," Nigel said. "We have uniforms inside his house and office now who can't seem to locate any digital devices—no laptop, phone. The last ping of his mobile was at his address. Do you know where else he may have kept that sort of thing?"

"The laptop and phone were always either at his house or his work," Boycie said as Precious sat and sobbed, Bach coming forward to pat her shoulder. "Maybe in his car?"

"They've looked. Nothing."

"I don't know, then." Boycie scrubbed a palm over his stubble.

"Do you know of anyone who may have a grudge against Alice *and* Everett?" Nigel asked.

"No bloody idea." Boycie shook his head. "You said body parts. What the hell's going on?"

Nigel stood. Closed his eyes while he pinched the bridge of his nose, looking like he'd rather be anywhere but here, working this case. "His head and arm were in the back garden at his father's place. There's a bricked-up outhouse which will be checked as it didn't look right to me. You knew Everett as kids. Did the outhouse ever have a door?"

"No idea," Boycie said.

"Right, err, we'll let you get back to sleep."

"Sleep?" Precious said, hoping her nose and eyes were red. "How can I sleep when my boyfriend's dead?"

"Hmm. We'll be off then."

Nigel and Bach walked out.

Precious waited for the front door to shut before she whispered, "I wonder where Colin is, that DS."

"Dunno. He might be at Roach's house." Boycie leaned back. "Do you think we'll get away with it?"

"I bloody hope so. Seeing George with that machete... Fucked if I want him using it on me."

"He must have believed us, else he'd never have killed Roach."

George had said the CCTV footage in this area had gone missing, the whole day wiped out. She hadn't asked who'd done it, just nodded, accepting everything he'd told her about creating a believable alibi. Not that she needed a lesson in doing that. She'd already created the perfect alibi for Alice's murder.

If she ever got caught for that, she dreaded to think what George would do to her.

"How long do we wait before we go after Kayla and Edna?" she asked.

"We'll play it by ear."

She nodded. Maybe they should let the dust settle, regardless of her being impatient to get all the loose ends tied up. Rome wasn't built in a day, and it was better to plan this properly than jump in without thinking it through.

She imagined someone finding Edna, ages after her death. No fucker ever went round to see her, so it wouldn't be until she smelled that someone would maybe notice she hadn't been around for a while. And as for Kayla, well, killing her in her flat would pose a problem—a Cooper-sized problem.

Precious sighed and smiled at Boycie. "Fancy a shag?"

Chapter Thirty-Seven

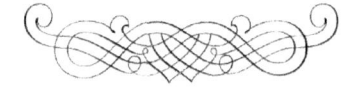

After a few days of keeping away, what with the police interest at the brothel, the twins had decided it was time to let Widow know the score. The Orange Lantern wasn't as George had expected. He was used to seeing the parlour at the back of The Angel, understated, tasteful. But this? It was like every years-gone-by knocking shop he'd seen on the telly. The living room—or receiving room as Precious had called it—fucking hell... Gaudy flock wallpaper in dark red, the sofas the same colour. It gave off a seedy vibe, the black silk curtains with swags at the tops something from a historical novel, and as for Widow...

He glanced over at her where she stood in the doorway, one foot in the room, the other in the hallway, as if she'd frozen in shock at the sight of the twins in her establishment. He'd asked Precious to go and collect her from the office so they could have a little chat. No punters sat waiting, so now was the perfect time to explain how things would work.

Widow raised her perfectly plucked eyebrows and plonked her hands on her hips. Her dress, the same weird flock as the wallpaper, except in green, had an actual bustle at the back as though she'd stepped out of olden-day times into today. Lace ruffles at her neck, and a godawful black velvet hat with a peacock feather on it.

"What the fuck's going on for *you two* to be here?" she said, her accent rough as arseholes. "I know who you are, but what's the problem?"

She was aware Everett had died—or Roach as she knew him. So was most of the country, seeing as a dismembered head and arm tended to make a good news story, plus the discovery of a skeleton in an outhouse, Everett's dad arrested, but she'd clearly assumed things would continue as normal, seeing as the tenancy with the estate agent was in her name. They'd draw a new one up for her because…

"We put in an offer for the house which was accepted," George said. "If you want to still work here and do whatever it is you do, then we're fine with that, but if you don't, I'm sure it won't take us long to find someone else."

Widow nodded. "I'll stay, thank you. I didn't build this place up to have it whipped away from me."

"If the Old Bill ever find out what goes on here and contact us, we'll deny all knowledge. You'll have to pay us rent, the bills, and protection money."

"How much?"

"Five grand a month should cover everything."

She nodded; so this place clearly brought in a wedge if she could afford the payment. She probably took money off the women who rented the rooms, maybe even dabbled with punters herself from time to time, and if she hadn't, she'd perhaps have to start. Precious had said Everett paid her and Widow to do their jobs. George and Greg had already discussed this, and they'd be paying them, too, because they wanted any intel they could pick up here.

George stuck his hand out. Widow did the same, and they shook on it.

"Fuck us about, and you know what's coming," he said.

Widow nodded. "We'll have no problems if you leave me to run this place like Everett did." She smiled and backed into the hallway, then swept off in her ancient gown.

"Fucking weirdo," George muttered.

Greg laughed. "She's a rare one, I'll say that for her."

"She's nice," Precious said. "She won't muck you about."

George scowled. "Best she doesn't."

The doorbell rang, and Precious nipped out to answer it. She came back with a woman, sex on legs quite frankly, and it took George a second to get himself together. Jessica Rabbit, that's what she reminded him of, although her hair wasn't red but black. This had to be that Goddess bird.

He cleared his throat. "Evening."

He nodded at her and walked out, leaving the house before he made a prick of himself. There was something about her that had reduced him to feeling like a teenager again.

Fuck that. Women are nothing but trouble.

He waited for Greg in the BMW, his brother more than likely being polite and covering up for George's swift exit by making out he was ill or something.

There was one more stop to make, then they could go home.

Wigs and beards on, the BMW switched for their little white van with an electrician's logo on the side, the twins walked up the garden path. To say the reason for this visit had come as a bit of a shock a few days ago was an understatement. They'd had to wait before they could come—too many nosy pigs around—and Janine had said it was probably best they pretended to be here on a job, just in case officers were watching the house.

She opened the door, letting them in, leading the way to Colin's kitchen. *Colin*, for fuck's sake, a straight-as-an-arrow man now intent on getting justice for his wife's murder. That or to be involved in taking other scummy cunts down so he felt like he was doing something worthwhile. Janine had assured them that despite Colin disliking bent coppers, him now wanting to be one was because the same drive that had pushed her was now pushing him.

Yeah, anger needed an outlet, and if working for the twins kept Colin focused, then that had to be a good thing. George had reminded her, though, that she'd also recommended Flint, and look what a shitshow that had turned out to be.

She'd told him to fuck off.

Colin sat in an armchair by the window, his face haggard. He'd lost a lot of weight in the week since his missus had copped it, and he fiddled with a bright-pink stress ball, rhythmically squeezing. He stared outside, maybe at their van, maybe at the bird over the road doing a bit of pruning, but George knew he wasn't seeing anything. It got you like that, grief, encasing you in an opaque bubble that prevented you from viewing things clearly ever again.

"Are you sure about this, Colin?" Greg asked, sitting on the sofa. "It's bloody hard work, and not being funny, mate, but you don't exactly look in tiptop condition."

"I'll be all right. I just need something to keep me going." He pulled his attention from the window and stared at Greg. "Just tell me what to do, and I'll do it."

George didn't like the sound of that. Colin was too resigned. No fire in his belly. "You don't sound up to snuff, pal, sorry."

Janine's mouth dropped open. "Give him a fucking chance. The proper anger hasn't come yet."

George nodded. "All right, but we can't afford any liabilities. So long as that's clear from the start…"

Colin swung his gaze to him. "I keep thinking about her, lying on the floor, trying to fight him off. She had his DNA under her fingernails, you know, but he's not in the system, so he's still out there, could be doing it to someone else. He tore her down there, where he forced it in…" He took a deep breath. "And I'm telling you now, I've never wanted to kill *anyone* more than I do him. I can see it, taste it, hear him screaming. I want you to find him—Nigel's stretched too thin with Everett's case and that bloody skeleton, so I'm going back to work tomorrow to take that over while he concentrates on my wife's. If I hear any info, I'll tell you. If I find out who it is, I'll ring you before the police have time to round him up. I don't want him going to prison."

George nodded again. "Right. We'll be in touch." He smiled at Janine. "We'll send Colin's burner and whatever round to yours for you to pass it on. Best we don't send it here, not if any police are out there. Look after yourself, Colin. We'll do our best to find who did it."

In the van, Greg driving, George let out a long sigh. They'd already put men out on the streets, asking if there was any intel floating around about a rapist. A few snitches had agreed to keep their ears to the ground, but that might not be enough. That woman's killer might very well walk free.

Chapter Thirty-Eight

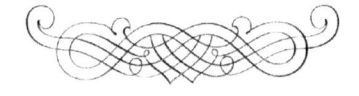

August was about the right time to get things moving. Weeks had passed since Roach's head and arm had been discovered. She sighed, her long shift over. Listening in for the twins was harder work than she'd imagined. Staying alert, watching people's faces... At three a.m., she said goodbye to Widow and left the Orange Lantern, having changed into workout gear so she could jog back to the flat, her dress and high-heeled shoes in her backpack. She'd been thinking about Kayla and Edna all night, the need to get rid of them a gnawing set of teeth in her gut. Boycie had put off talking about it ever since Roach had died, saying he was just chuffed the twins believed them, so he didn't want to rock the boat, at least not until Everett's estate had been sorted.

Boycie had been twiddling his thumbs with fuck all to do except a few carpentry jobs. The twins now owned the brothel, the drugs angle had been removed from the equation, and the fake financial consultancy business just sat there doing nothing. He'd grumbled about not thinking things through fully, completely forgetting Roach had paid them in wedges of cash and could no longer do so. They'd ended up being worse off instead of coining in the riches they'd imagined. Precious had worked that out, back in the planning stage, but her need for Roach to die had overridden her desire for cash. Anyway, the house and flats would come Boycie's way soon.

A breeze whooshed against her face. She plodded on in the darkness, upping her pace, checking all the usual places where CCTV could be mounted. As always on this route, there was sod all, but you could never be too careful, could you. The day you decided to inject someone with a too much heroin might be the day a new camera went up.

She smiled, her steps light as she nipped into an alley down the back of people's homes. Bungalows. Easy to break into. She'd been here several nights lately, just staring through the slight gap in the curtains into Edna's bedroom, watching the woman breathe in her sleep.

Later, Precious left the back garden and continued home. Edna would see the light of another day. But not for much longer. Once Precious had all her T's crossed, there'd be no stopping her.

The loose ends needed tying up once and for all.

To be continued in *Recite,*
The Cardigan Estate 33

Printed in Great Britain
by Amazon